THE HALLOWEEN GANG

A HALLOWEEN TO REMEMBER

JEFFREY JANAKUS

BEAVER'S POND
PRESS

Edited by Wendy Weckwerth
Cover Illustration by Deborah Garcia

ISBN 13: 978-1-64343-928-0
Library of Congress Catalog Number: 2019906406

Printed in the United States of America
First Printing: 2020
24 23 22 21 20   5 4 3 2 1

Cover and interior design by Dan Pitts

BEAVER'S POND
PRESS

Beaver's Pond Press, Inc.
939 Seventh Street West
Saint Paul, MN 55102
(952) 829-8818
www.BeaversPondPress.com

To order, visit www.ItascaBooks.com or call (800) 901-3480. Reseller discounts available.

Contact Jeffrey Janakus at www.JeffreyJanakus.com to inquire about speaking engagements, school visits, book club discussions, and interviews.

To my beautiful wife, my amazing children,
and all others who love Halloween as much as we do—
particularly, the awesome spectacle that is trick-or-treating.

1

Trick~or~Treating, Last Year

"What a *great plan*—lightening the load by stashing half our loot in the dugout! Would've been hard lugging all our candy around the whole night. Unloading halfway through made it *way* easier to maneuver and allowed us to snag a world-record haul—worked out fantabulously!" proclaims Mooch as he raises both arms in triumph. He and the rest of the gang—Mike, Phil, and Cruz—are heading back toward their houses, ending what all of them are classifying as a highly successful night of trick-or-treating.

Mooch is dressed as Al Capone (portraying the character from *The Untouchables*, a new movie he's heard much about and is eager to see), and this year, amazingly enough, he's managed to keep his costume clean and without rips, tears, or even scuffs—a feat the others would attest to as being an unprecedented accomplishment.

"Yeah, I'm not sure you would've made it all the way otherwise," responds Phil.

Phil is dressed as Ferris Bueller and to the dismay of his cohorts, he's been continuously imitating the lead character by singing out loudly "Chicka-chicka!" from the movie's theme song and "Danke schoen!" from the signature downtown Chicago parade scene while strutting around in an uncharacteristically dramatic fashion all night long.

"He *would not* have," adds Cruz, smirking. "You would've been *begging* me to carry your stuff for the past hour," he continues, glancing back at Mooch.

Mooch nods in agreement with Cruz's assessment. He can't help but admit his habitual laziness would've undoubtedly emerged under such circumstances.

Cruz is dressed as the Karate Kid and has thus far refused repeated requests from his buddies to mimic the well-known moves from the film—including "Wax on, wax off," "Paint the fence," and "Sand the floor." Feeling compelled to give the movie some love and take advantage of a rare opportunity to mess with Cruz, Mooch and Phil can't resist calling him "Daniel-san." They also keep reenacting the famed crane-kick move that earned the main character victory at the end of the movie. Their ongoing antics have Cruz wondering if maybe one of them would've been better suited for the costume.

"It was a good night, a great night! It was a masterfully developed and perfectly executed plan, boys. High fives!" summarizes Mike as he one by one slaps the others' hands, held high in the air. "Now let's go retrieve that loot and head to my house to celebrate!"

He's dressed in a naval pilot's flight suit (portraying Maverick from *Top Gun*) and has thoroughly enjoyed repeating the movie's famous line, "I feel the need, the need for *speed*!"

Feeling exuberant about the night's accomplishments and eager to enjoy mass quantities of candy while rehashing their experiences, they begin to walk swiftly back to the location of their stashed loot—the first-base dugout of the town's Little League baseball field.

The year is 1987. Now in the sixth grade, the gang has been an inseparable group since the last of the quartet, Cruz, moved to their town in east-central Texas over three years ago.

Mike Hendricks is the leader. He's eleven years old, tall and slender, and has short, wavy, dark-brown hair and blue eyes. He's intelligent (getting mostly As, and a few Bs, in school) and athletic (the starting shortstop and pitcher on the Little League team and one of the best basketball players in town). All the kids and parents in the neighborhood know him to be an upstanding, honorable young man.

Mooch Henderson, whose given name is Oscar (only his mom, teachers at school, and, on occasion, other adults in the neighborhood call him that), is the jokester of the gang. He's eleven years old, of medium height, chubby, and has buzz-cut sandy blonde hair and blue eyes. He likes to eat, isn't particularly interested in applying himself at school, is athletic in ability (the starting catcher on the Little League team) but not in physicality (being overweight and lazy), and is easily agitated and frightened.

Phil Mendelson is the brainiac planner and problem-solver of the gang. He's eleven years old, short and skinny, has short, straight black hair and brown eyes, and wears thick-lensed glasses with black frames. He's exceptionally intelligent, quick-witted, and sarcastic. Though he's on the Little League team, he isn't particularly athletic, and mostly sits the bench—preferring to assist the coach with game strategy over playing.

Cruz Rivera is the gang's muscle, their protector. He's called "Brooz" (short for Bruiser) by the younger classes and rival groups due to his intimidating presence. He just turned twelve years old, is tall and big, has a wavy black mullet and brown eyes. He's strong and quiet (preferring to talk only when necessary) and shares in Mike's motto of doing things "by the book." He is an average outfielder on the Little League team, but is more adept at, and has thus been focusing more on, football.

In excited anticipation of retrieving the stowed half of their candy, the gang picks up the pace from a brisk walk to swift jog and accelerates as quickly as possible down Enchantress Way. Approaching the end of the street, they hear a loud and strange noise up ahead near the Clarks' house—a house all the kids in the neighborhood believe to be haunted. After years of listening to and repeating the countless stories of horror surrounding this house, any inexplicable noise coming from its general vicinity is cause for immediate alarm.

The instant they hear the noise, each member of the gang stops dead in his tracks. Their breathing stops so as not to make a sound, their eyes and ears open wide on high alert, and their arms extend out into the dark night air, attempting to sense any and all vibrations. After several moments of remaining still and hearing only silence, they let out a collective deep breath and look at each other nervously before reaching a nonverbal consensus to forge ahead.

3

They proceed forward slowly and cautiously, being extra careful to make as little noise as possible.

As they reach the near corner of the ornate but deteriorating black-iron fence that lines the front yard's perimeter, clouds have started to accumulate in front of tonight's nearly full moon, creating ominous shadows on the pavement that extend to spooky figures cascading up the sides of the white house and onto its dark-shingled roof. With the boys' fears building, all senses are heightened—looking, listening, feeling, and now smelling and tasting the air for the slightest disturbance in the darkened stillness and silence. As they pass before the half-open front gate—now leaning away from the support pillar, supported only by the bottom hinge with the top hinge broken and disengaged—they briefly peer into the Clarks' yard to see only pitch-black darkness. They slowly turn their heads away from the opening to continue forward—when suddenly a loud bark from a neighboring dog bellows in the night sky. Mooch, in the rear of the group, is so alarmed that he jumps (as much as he's able to actually jump) directly into Cruz, who's in front of him. This move triggers a chain reaction of Cruz slamming into Phil, Phil crashing into Mike, and all falling to the ground.

Mike rolls to his side and winces in pain as he rubs his right hip. He slowly rises to his feet and looks back at the others as if to say—

"What the heck, guys?!" groans Phil, lying on his back in agony and holding his left shoulder.

Cruz sits up, cradles his bruised right knee with one hand, and answers Phil's question by simply pointing at Mooch with an aggravated look.

"Sorry, guys. I just got a little scared by that dogs' bark," responds Mooch.

"A little?!" retorts Phil.

Cruz slowly stands as an annoyed Mike half-heartedly helps Mooch to his feet in his now torn and scuffed costume.

Staring at Mooch with disdain, Phil is the last to rise, gingerly holding his shoulder with one hand while carefully adjusting his glasses with the other. "So much for keeping your costume clean for the first time ever. The streak is still intact."

With their pains easing, they dust themselves off while exchanging a few more insults, directed mostly at Mooch, and then collectively agree to dispense with the conversation and carry on. Turning to proceed forward, they're startled by a pair of boys who seemingly appear out of nowhere. Blocking their path are the detestable Josh Pealy and Bobby Poda. Panicked, Mooch turns around, contemplating running in the opposite direction. Before he can act, he's confronted by the other half of this most-hated foursome, Rob Broadway and Travis Bennett, cutting off their potential escape route.

Josh, Bobby, Rob, and Travis form the crew that has been the arch nemesis of Mike's Gang for years. They're also in the sixth grade and are mean, vindictive, and jealous of the gang's expert skill at consistently planning and executing highly successful trick-or-treating outings.

Josh is the group leader. He's just turned twelve years old, is tall and big (nearly as big as Cruz), and has short, curly red hair, freckles, and blue eyes. He's malicious, vengeful, and deceitful (being cunningly adept at convincing parents and teachers he's a fine and upstanding young boy, while opportunistically bullying and terrorizing as many kids as possible in the neighborhood and at school). He's on one of the town's football teams, but only occasionally plays; athleticism isn't his strong suit.

Bobby Poda is Josh's right-hand thug. He's eleven years old, of medium height and average build, has straight, light-brown hair and brown eyes, and wears sports glasses secured by an elastic band. Bobby's a mischievously intelligent street fighter who loyally carries out all orders delivered by Josh. He's also on a football team, but rarely sees playing time, being the slowest kid in the neighborhood.

Rob Broadway is eleven years old, of medium height and build, and tightly curled black hair paired with big brown eyes. He submissively goes along with whatever Josh and Bobby command (rarely having an opinion of his own). Rob is the starting tailback on the number-one football team in town and the best sprinter on the track team—unquestionably the fastest kid in the neighborhood. He sometimes empathizes with Mike and his gang, particularly when he feels Josh is being excessively unfair or overzealous in his cruelty toward them, but has never had the courage to speak his mind, fearing Josh's wrath.

The final member of the crew is Travis Bennett. He's eleven years old, very short and skinny, and has wavy, sandy-blonde hair and green eyes. Travis is gullible. He's only a member of the crew because, first, he desperately wants to be, and second, he fulfills the key role of guinea pig for the group. He often tries to provide input, but his attempts are never acknowledged by the others.

"Okay, nerds, time to hand over your candy," demands Josh, dressed as Hulk Hogan and pointing a slingshot loaded with a rock about the size of a golf ball directly at Mike.

Mike looks at Josh's other hand and sees it's holding two additional rocks of similar size, ready for a quick reload. He knows full well that Josh isn't bluffing, that he'll fire to achieve his goal if he has to. He looks around at the rest of Josh's Crew and finds them all in similar positions, ready to fire and ready to quickly reload.

"No!" screams Mooch, his heart nearly pounding out of his chest, half out of fear and half out of anger. "You can't, you won't take our candy! It's ours!"

With the slingshots of Rob (dressed up as Houston Oilers quarterback Warren Moon) and Travis (Crocodile Dundee) now pointed directly at Mooch, Josh glances in their direction and replies, "Yes, we can. And, yes, we will. Hand it over now and you won't be harmed. Don't, and we'll pummel you with rocks first and then take it."

Cruz advances threateningly toward Bobby, but thinks better of it and eases off as Bobby, in his Robocop costume, quickly pulls back, tightening the tension of his slingshot. Dejected, defeated, outgunned, and still recovering from their domino fall, the gang has no choice but to hand over their bags. Each of them comes to the same aggravating realization: Josh and his crew are going to *undeservingly* and *maliciously* reap the benefits of this night's amazing candy haul, and they can do nothing to stop it. As a minuscule consolation, they're somewhat comforted by the thought that at least half of their candy is still stashed away for a later retrieval.

"Come on, let's go! Throw your bags over to me. Now!" demands Josh as the wind suddenly gusts from the Clarks' yard, blowing leaves, sticks, and random candy wrappers scampering along the ground through the group.

The gang looks at one another completely dispirited and then each slowly and methodically begins to remove the well-stocked bag from his shoulder. As they swing them backward in preparation for tossing them to their adversaries, a loud *aaaah-woooh* booms from the Clarks' front yard—their swinging bags instantly stop. With the wind and tumbling debris increasing, both groups remain frozen, intently listening as the *aaaah-wooooooooh* again booms, continuing this time for several seconds. Being well versed in the countless horror stories surrounding the Clarks' house, the collective group is blanketed by an intense sense of fear. A few more seconds pass before a louder *AAAAH-WOOOH!* bellows from the Clarks' front yard. That one sounds closer than the previous two! With the hair on the heads of each boy now standing straight up and goose bumps covering every square inch of exposed skin, they remain motionless, locked in absolute terror. As several more seconds pass in silence, the group begins to think that perhaps the worst is behind them. They release a collective exhale of relief before a deafening *AAAAAAAH-WOOOOOOH!* thunders through the air. A *whoosh* simultaneously whistles violently through the group—another gust of wind carrying even more debris that forcefully hits the boys' bodies. Having seen and heard enough, Josh and his goons immediately drop their slingshots to their sides and run away as fast as possible in terror.

"The Clarks' ghost! Let's go, guys! Run!" yells Mike as he sprints in the direction opposite of where Josh and his crew are headed. Cruz runs at his side, followed closely by Phil, with a laboring Mooch trailing farther behind.

Reaching the end of the block, now presumably clear of any harm, Mike and Cruz stop and each bends at the waist, hands to his knees, gasping for air. A few moments later Phil jogs up to the others and crashes to the ground in exhaustion. Bringing up the rear many moments later is Mooch, working his way gradually from slow jog, to walk, to crawl, to lying on his back facing the night sky and gasping for oxygen.

"What . . . was . . . that?" he asks, taking huge gulps of air in between each word.

"Don't know . . . good part is . . . we didn't have to give up our . . . candy," says Mike, also struggling to breathe.

"Fortuitous," declares Phil.

Cruz shakes his head in agreement and then comments, "You've been dying to use that word from last week's vocab challenge, haven't you?"

Phil grins and shakes his head affirmatively.

After taking a couple more minutes to catch their breath, they all turn and begin walking toward the baseball field.

"Let's go get our stashed candy and go home," Mike suggests. "That's enough excitement for tonight."

The others nod in agreement and then slowly march off together, now eager to end the night on a positive note.

"Argh! Those scumbags!" shouts Mooch as he, Mike, Cruz, and Phil gaze in shock at the site of their candy stash. The container sits open in the dugout, dimly lit by moonlight peeking through semi-cloudy skies.

"Thanks, suckers!" reads a lone note left in the container. Clearly the work of Josh and his goons, the gang looks at each other in sickened befuddlement as their mood slowly transforms from shock to disappointment to anger. Mike and Cruz are angry because of the maliciousness and cruelty of the act. Phil is also angry, but more preoccupied with feeling conflictedly ashamed at being outwitted by Josh's Crew, while impressed by how masterfully it was achieved. Mooch is the angriest, virtually in a rage, at not having *all* of his candy to enjoy over the coming days.

"They stole our stash!" he shouts with his face flushed red as he tears his Capone-style fedora off his head and throws it against the dugout wall. "And, if not for the Clarks' ghost, those dirtbags would've gotten *every piece* of our candy! This is HORRIBLE! We *must* get revenge! This means *war*!"

The others agree, but insist that it must be done "their way" via their signature meticulous planning and flawless execution. After several minutes of heated discussion, they convince Mooch that retribution can't be impulsive; it must be calculated and carefully timed. Josh is clever, plus he'll be on the alert for immediate attempts at revenge. So, any immediate plans would surely backfire, creating additional aggravation and disappointment.

They agree that word of this despicable incident cannot, under any circumstance, get out to the neighborhood. That would tarnish the impeccable trick-or-treating reputation they've worked so hard to build. They make a pact not to speak a word of tonight's mistreatment outside their foursome. Knowing that Josh will never risk his reputation (more appropriately, *façade*) of being a straitlaced kid in the eyes of the adults in the neighborhood, the gang is confident the secret won't be advertised by Josh or his cohorts.

Phil vows to get to work on the revenge plan tomorrow as they all head back to Mike's house to enjoy what candy remains and to lament further on how they were the victims of the biggest Halloween heist ever.

2

Best Time of Year

It's again the exciting time of the year when trick-or-treating complete-ly consumes all facets of the gang's lives. No matter where they are or what they're doing, their minds are preoccupied with planning this year's campaign.

"This is the *best* time of year. Candy out the wazoo, costumes, ex-citement, adventure—I LOVE IT!" Mooch tells Mike as they weave their way through the other kids walking down the school hallway on their way to lunch. "I know Christmas is king with the big presents, cookies, pies, and all, but you can't deny that Halloween is a very close second. Thanksgiving is also great with the continuous eating—turkey, mashed potatoes, pie—but it can't compare to the lasting enjoyment of Halloween, eating tons of candy for days! I just can't understand why they don't give us the day of and the day after Halloween off to get ready and recover?"

Mike smiles. "Yeah, all good points, but I'm not sure everyone else feels as strongly as you do about Halloween."

"You mean as strongly as *we* do. I guess so, but how can you NOT love this holiday?! Free candy, free chocolate—as much as you can car-ry! And, *and*, you get to dress up however you want. It's *the* greatest American pastime, bigger than baseball, hot dogs, and apple pie and all that. Camaraderie and sharing mixed with surprise and fright—Hal-loween has it all! It's the only day of the year when people are just as likely to scare the bejesus out of you as they are to give you mass quantities of scrumptious candy! It should be a national holiday, no question. Days off should be given immediately, end of story."

"Hard to argue with that," Mike says with a laugh, playfully shoving Mooch into the doorjamb as they enter the lunchroom. Next year at this time they'll be eighth graders, the "big men on campus," just a year away from high school. "But I don't know if Halloween is bigger than baseball. Maybe tied?"

"No way. *Tied?!* Look, I like baseball too, but come on! Halloween! Candy!" replies Mooch staring intently at Mike with his arms extended out wide.

"Guys! We have *so much* to do. We *have* to get started TONIGHT!" says Phil, who's waiting inside the door. "They should really give us the day of Halloween off to prepare. Not enough time."

"Exactly!" Mooch exclaims. "Should be a national holiday, right?"

"For sure. We should start a petition. It should also always be on a Friday, that way we have the whole weekend to recover," responds Phil as the three of them continue toward their customary lunchroom table together.

"Ooh! I like that the sound of that. Two solid days of uninterrupted candy consumption. Yes!" replies Mooch, rubbing his hands together and licking his lips.

Now seated at their table, the trio unpacks their lunches and begins to rehash last year's tragic trick-or-treating fiasco. Although it was nearly one year ago, the agony of Josh and his crew stealing their stashed candy still stings as fiercely as it did that dreadful day. Mooch has been jolted awake several times recently after having nightmares about Josh stealing every piece of candy he's ever received and ever will receive in this life—a most terrifying thought. But the agony of defeat stings a little less at this particular moment as he focuses on something more important—digging through his lunch pack in search of the day's dessert.

"Found it! Come to papa!" yells Mooch as he finds the sweet treasure.

Phil's also had several nightmares about last year's embarrassing turn of events. His, however, are more focused on his frustration that they were—more specifically, that *he* was—outwitted by Josh and less on the loss of candy. Phil hates nothing more than being outsmarted.

He prides himself on developing meticulous, well-timed, airtight plans and expects himself to think of all possible snags, to be one step ahead of his foes at every turn.

"You better eat your sandwich first, Oscar. Don't want to get full on your dessert and skip the nutritious part of the meal," says Phil, waving his finger and mimicking Mooch's mom.

"Don't call me that!" retorts Mooch, staring back sternly at Phil.

Continuing to wave his finger at Mooch, Phil laughs and then takes a bite of his sandwich.

"Phil?! Stop it," demands Mike.

"No more!" exclaims Mooch continuing to stare sternly at Phil, still focused on the unwanted use of his given name.

"Did you use the *O-word* again?" asks Cruz of Phil as he joins the table. Mike shakes his head side to side and chuckles.

"Okay, Smoochy Smooch," replies Phil with a puckered face, making a kissing, smooching sound.

"Stop it, nerd," retorts Mooch.

"Okay, okay," concedes Phil with a giggle. He then turns his attention quickly back to the logistics of planning for the upcoming holiday. "But, guys, we have to, *absolutely have to,* meet TONIGHT. We're running out of time!"

"Payback is *way* overdue for those scumbags. We've waited *so* long for revenge. It's been *so* agonizing!" exclaims Mooch with his hands, grabbing the hair on his head in frustration.

"*So* agonizing. Been painful!" agrees Phil.

For the past year Mike has somehow managed to keep both Mooch and Phil from making haphazard attempts at retaliation against Josh's Crew. On several occasions the two have worked each other into a frenzy as they chaotically schemed extravagant payback scenarios—scenarios that, if not for Mike talking sense into them, undoubtedly would have ended in disappointment and embarrassment. But now the time for redemption is finally here, and they're all excited for revenge.

"My house. After school. Today," declares Mike.

The others nod in concurrence.

Then, as it often does, especially at this time of year, the conversation quickly shifts to candy. While thoroughly enjoying his Nestlé Crunch bar (having not yet touched or even unpacked any other items from his lunch), Mooch begins pontificating on his candy preferences.

"Any candy bar with chocolate, lots and lots of chocolate. Chocolate is everything, the only thing, when it comes to scrumptious snacks and desserts. Chocolate is the perfect combination of silky texture and sweetly goodness. All chocolates are welcome—dark, milk, and white—I don't discriminate. But I must say that milk chocolate is preferred when given the choice."

Eating their lunches in a more traditional order (sandwich and chips, then fruit, and dessert last) than Mooch's dessert-first approach, the others just shake their heads, having heard this speech many times before. As is customary, Mooch proceeds to his stock complaints about hard candy.

"If you suck on it like you're 'supposed' to," he says making a quotation gesture with his hands, "it takes too long. The experience and enjoyment are ruined by the boringness. But then if you bite it, it's gone quickly. The experience disappears in a fleeting moment—no enjoyment, just *poof,* gone. There's no 'sweet' spot with hard candy. It either takes so long you get distracted by other things and don't actually enjoy it or it's gone before you even get to give it a proper tasting. I just don't get it, at all."

Mooch continues as the others, currently more interested in their lunches, pay scant attention. "The grand master of BAD hard candy has got to be peppermint. It's like eating a hard block of toothpaste. Like eating a 'healthy' candy. Makes no sense. Gives candy a bad name."

Phil, who's okay with hard candy in some instances, shakes his head in disagreement. But as usual he refrains from arguing with Mooch, knowing it would only end in another drawn-out stalemate.

"Chewy candy has good flavor, but it's annoying because it sticks to your teeth," proclaims Mooch.

Phil joins in with a droning voice as Mooch delivers his signature line: "It slows your consumption rate way too much."

Mooch stands, raises his left hand into the air, places his right hand on his chest, and elevates his voice to declare, "The perfect candy bar is a candy bar that has a chocolate-chocolate-chip-cookie center, surrounded by a layer of thick chocolate custard infused with chocolate chips, and covered in a thick chocolate topping. . . Plus, the ultimate topper—an *edible* chocolate wrapper!"

They others laugh, having not heard the edible chocolate wrapper part before.

"And I would name it . . . the Moochocolate Bar!"

"Ha! Mooooch!" yells Phil.

Sitting down again, Mooch proudly concludes, "Because as you know, boys, any candy without chocolate—"

"Is NOT WORTHY OF MY TASTE BUDS!" exclaim all four in unison.

"My favorite's Kit Kat. It's like eating a *real* cookie candy bar," Mike chimes in. "I like chocolate too, but I like the vanilla cookie mixed in for some variety in flavor. My second choice has to be Twix—similar to Kit Kat, but with caramel added."

Just now getting to his sandwich and chips, Mooch says under his breath, "Also happens to be Lisa Heatherman's favorite."

Phil and Cruz chuckle.

Mike turns to Mooch and punches him in the arm.

"Ow! I was only joking," whimpers Mooch.

"I don't mind hard or chewy candy under the right circumstances, but it's not worth arguing about," says Phil to Mooch. Turning his attention to the entire group, he continues, "What I like best is mixing sweet candy with salty snacks. Like Cracker Jack or buttered popcorn combined with M&M's or gummy bears. Or saltines and peanut butter with Hershey's chocolate syrup on top—salty s'mores!"

Mike shivers making a face of disgust while Mooch grunts, "Ugh."

"You guys don't know what you're missing," declares Phil. "So good!"

"I like the M&M's part," concedes Mooch.

Cruz has never given a definitive answer about his candy preferences, but Mike is determined to get one this time. "Okay, today's the day, Cruz. What's your favorite?"

After taking a few moments to ponder, Cruz says with his typical minimalistic style, "I like the biggest ones, the most-filling ones."

"Come on! You can do better than that. Name a *candy*!" demands Mike.

"Yeah, that's lame," adds Phil.

"For sure. We're talking about *candy* here. This is serious, not to be taken lightly. Especially this time of year—you're tempting the Candy Gods into messing with us," adds Mooch. The term *Candy Gods* is used often by the gang to describe the karma that will inevitably ensue if one doesn't respect the sanctity of Halloween and the significance of trick-or-treating. The foursome often recollects fearful tales of when they didn't sufficiently respect the holiday. Sometimes their carelessness resulted in candy issues, several times in costume problems, and often in conflicts with Josh's Crew. Not provoking the Candy Gods is a matter the gang doesn't take lightly, for good reason.

"Well, not sure that Cruz not picking a candy counts as tempting the Candy Gods," Mike replies. He then turns back to Cruz, determined to get a meaningful response. "But come on, Cruz. Let's have it. Give us a *real* answer."

Cruz pauses to think again for a few moments and then reluctantly acknowledges, "I guess my favorite would be a milkshake or malt. Mega size. Preferably made with peanut butter and bananas. Fills me up and tastes good!"

While this is more than they've ever gotten out of him before, the others remain unsatisfied.

"That does sound good—I'd add some chocolate if I were you," states Mooch, now partially distracted, dreaming about how delicious a large chocolate–chocolate chip malt would be right about now. "But it's not a *candy*!"

After pausing once again, this time for several seconds, Cruz proclaims, "Well, if had to pick a candy bar, it would probably be Snickers because they carry the most bang for the buck."

"They really satisfy!" exclaims Phil as they all laugh together.

"Snickers are good," adds Mooch as he licks his lips.

"Yes!" Mike exclaims, smiling from ear to ear. "I knew we'd finally get it out of you!"

The conversation quickly shifts again as Phil reminds everyone that they shall not eat the "forbidden and taboo" candy, Clark Bars. "You risk colossal wrath from the Candy Gods if you partake. Way too risky," he says with a touch of fear in his voice.

"Definitely," Mike and Cruz reply in unison.

Mooch nods in agreement but remains silent. He can't resist the chocolaty goodness of Clark Bars and as such, eats them in secrecy. Risking the Candy Gods' wrath is worth the reward for his taste buds.

Moving past the Clark Bar minefield, Mooch turns the conversation back to lamenting the loss of so many good candy bars in last year's debacle. He begins by ranting about half of their candy being stolen and drones on for several minutes about how evil and awful Josh and his goons are and how the gang must have revenge.

"Pealy," grumbles Mooch under his breath. To Mooch, Josh's last name is the most appallingly awful and horrible term imaginable. It represents all that is evil and nasty. He often says that if you could take all the curse words in the world and combine them into one super curse word, its meaning would pale in comparison to *Pealy*.

As they head off to the playground for the balance of the lunch period, Mike reminds the others about the meeting after school at his house to begin the planning for this years' trick-or-treat route (TOTR for short—pronounced *toter*). They collectively vow once again that this year they will not be careless. This year they'll develop a rock-solid plan and execute it perfectly—crossing every *t* and dotting every *i*, overlooking nothing. They must succeed, they will succeed, they *cannot* fail. It's a matter of life and death.

3

Lisa and Mike Trick~or~Treating?

Having just finished the rest of lunch period outside, Mike and Mooch head to their lockers to gather the materials they need for their next class.

"Tonight is the start of the reckoning. Payback time is coming for Pealy and his pack of goons. BIG TIME!" exclaims Mooch. "Oh, crap! I forgot. I have to finish my English paper—it's due next period!"

"What? How can you finish a paper with less than five minutes until class starts? Won't Mrs. Stevenson ask for it right at the beginning of class?" replies Mike, confused.

"Yeah, she will. But I do this all the time. I'm almost done, just have to finish the conclusion, no big deal. Gotta go, buddy!" says Mooch as he shuts his locker and hurries off to class.

Mike laughs to himself as he buries his head in his metal locker, located on the top tier of the long row. He grabs his mathematics text-book and spiral notebook and then backs his head out of his locker, grabs the door, and swings it closed.

"BOO!" shouts a voice, startling Mike, causing him to jump.

"Ha! Gotcha!" continues the voice that he now recognizes as Lisa Heatherman's. "Finally, you're not with your boys—sorry, your *gang*. You guys are inseparable. So cute."

"Crap! You scared the bejesus out of me," says Mike, his heart now racing. "Yeah, we tend to stick together. Most of the time."

He's nervous and his heart is racing because he's been startled, but more so because he's now talking to Lisa Heatherman, one of the prettiest girls in the school (certainly the prettiest in the seventh grade) and, in Mike's estimation, the prettiest girl in the entire town. He has liked Lisa ever since she moved to town in fourth grade, but he's always been too shy to show it.

With both their last names starting with "He" and many teachers seating their students in alphabetical order, they often sit next to or near each other in class. Over the three years since she moved to town, they've developed a playful rapport, but Mike still gets nervous around her and often can't think of anything to say. Thankfully, Lisa isn't shy, never seems nervous, and is never at a loss for words—particularly around Mike. She has liked Mike ever since the first time she set eyes on him her first day at school. He was wearing a bright-red Windbreaker that perfectly complemented his big, bright-blue eyes. Among his friends, Mike downplays his interest in Lisa and her interest in him, but his friends know better—their attraction to each other is obvious to anyone remotely paying attention. Lisa is less worried about others noticing their mutual affection—she knows and is flattered that Mike likes her and relishes every opportunity to flirt with him.

"So, you and your boys, your *gang*, have big plans for trick-or-treating again this year?" asks Lisa, twirling strands of her long brown hair in between and around her fingers.

"Yeah . . . you know . . . It's all about the quest for um, for ah, for trying to gather as much candy as possible. And having as much fun as possible doing it," replies Mike, still nervous and now staring into Lisa's beautiful brown eyes. "We spend the whole year planning—and then we have a blast trick-or-treating. It's awesome!"

"Well, about that . . . I wanted to ask you something . . . I was wondering if maybe you wanted to change things up a little this year?" she asks with a smile that shows off her sparkling white teeth.

"Change things up?"

"Yeah, change things up," she replies in a deepened voice, imitating Mike. "How?"

"Well, I'm wondering if maybe you'd like to go with *me* this year. Instead of your gang?" she asks, her voice cracking slightly with excitement and nervousness.

Mike freezes, equally surprised and flattered by her request. Mesmerized by her beauty, he takes in the subtle aroma of her perfume or lotion or whatever's making her smell so good. After a few moments of silence, he snaps out of his trance and begins to sweat in a panic. He fears he's taken too long to reply and is now embarrassing himself. Collecting himself, he replies, "Uh. Yeah. Sure, that would be great!"

Relieved, she says in her typical calm-and-cool manner, "Great, it's settled then. You and I trick-or-treating together. Looking forward to learning all your tricks—and treats. It's going to be a blast!"

She starts to walk away, but abruptly turns back to Mike and asks, "Oh yeah, I almost forgot. What're you going as? What's your costume?"

"Oh, uh, I think I'm going as Superman," a distracted Mike replies, his mind overwhelmed as he attempts to grasp what's happening.

"That's perfect! I was planning to go as Wonder Woman. See you later, Mikey," she says as she turns and strolls away.

Wonder Woman, wow! thinks Mike as he watches every elegant step Lisa takes to reach the end of the hallway before disappearing around a corner. He feels euphoric. Lisa Heatherman has just asked *him* to trick-or-treat with *her! Wow! Wow!* Questions and random thoughts now start to race through his mind. *Is this a date? No, it's not a date, right? But maybe it is a date? How and where will we meet? Will we hold hands? No, you can't hold hands and carry your trick-or-treating bag, right? Do I carry her bag for her? Probably, but maybe not. Will my costume be good enough? What will her costume look like?* And on and on.

He's excited and nervous at the same time—at a level he's never experienced. All those times in the batter's box needing to get a hit, all those times needing to make a big play to get out of the inning, all those times needing to drain a shot at the end of a basketball game—none felt as pressure packed as this monumental moment in his life.

Shaking his head vigorously from side to side in an attempt to stop his mind from racing at light speed, Mike slowly collects himself. As the gravity of the situation sinks in, his emotions transform from excitement to panic as quickly as his mind was racing just a moment ago.

Did I really just accept Lisa's invitation to trick-or-treat with her? Did I really just forget about my commitment to the gang? How did this happen?

RING! sounds the bell.

Crap! I'm late!

Mike runs down the hallway toward his next class. *The gang won't like this, not at all, not one bit! They'll never forgive me if I pick trick-or-treating with Lisa over them—especially this year, the year with so much at stake.* As he approaches the classroom, he realizes he has a problem, a really big dilemma, now.

4

Planning Meeting 1

Mike sits alone in his backyard clubhouse deliberating his sticky predicament. The ten-foot by ten-foot clubhouse that he helped his dad build last summer is the gang's primary hangout. It's clad in light, brownish-gray cedar siding with a dark shake-shingle roof, matching his house. The interior walls are unfinished, leaving exposed two-by-fours that are decorated with assorted sports posters and cheap memorabilia. From the rafters hangs an old chandelier that previously lived in Mike's kitchen. It washes the dusty dark-brown commercial-grade carpet flooring in a dim amber light. Furnished with four old kitchen chairs, his grandpa's antique wooden drafting table and metal stool, and a worn-out dark-brown suede recliner purchased at a garage sale, the clubhouse provides a safe and comfortable refuge for the gang.

His thoughts shift frantically back and forth between contemplating how he's going to tell his friends (they *won't* approve) and wondering if he can somehow cancel with Lisa (surely, she'll be eternally angry). The more he thinks about it, the more confused and frustrated he becomes. Locked in a mental stalemate, he resigns himself to the fact this won't get worked out today. He forces himself to focus on the TOTR, hoping that somehow it will still be relevant to his trick-or-treating this year.

Phil and Cruz show up at Mike's house first. As his mom opens the door, Phil announces, "Hello, Mrs. Hendricks, we're here to see Mike."

"Well hello, boys. How are you?" asks Mrs. Hendricks in her typical jovial fashion.

"We're doing great!" says Phil. "Halloween is almost here."

"Yes, it is—how fun! Mike is out back in the clubhouse waiting for you boys."

"Thanks, Mrs. Hendricks," says Phil as he and Cruz walk through the sliding-glass door at the back of the kitchen and head toward the clubhouse.

Mooch arrives a couple minutes later and is carrying a family-size bag of Doritos. "Hello, Mrs. Hendricks," he says as she opens the front door. "I'm here for the big meeting in the clubhouse."

"Hello, Oscar, how are you doing this evening?"

"Uh," replies Mooch, disappointed she called him by his given name, but not surprised. Adults often ignore his preferred moniker. "I'm doing good, I guess . . . I'm happy the trick-or-treating season is here, it's the best time of year. How are you doing this evening?"

"*Well.*"

"Huh?"

"You're doing *well*, not *good.*"

"Oh, yeah, I'm doing WELL!"

"That's better. Thank you for asking, I'm also doing *well*," she says with a chuckle.

Mooch nods and then shifts his attention to the wonderful aroma emanating throughout the house, "Mmmm. Something smells delicious. What are you making for dinner, Mrs. Hendricks?"

"Lasagna."

"Lasagna. Yum." Mooch inhales deeply, taking in as much of the wonderful scent as possible. He then moves toward the sliding glass door and says. "Good to see you, Mrs. Hendricks. I'm off to see Mikey."

"Okay, Mooch. Have fun, be safe."

Happy she used his preferred name this time, Mooch crosses the yard and enters the clubhouse while shoveling a handful of Doritos into his mouth. "What's up, boys?" he asks in a muffled and hardly understandable voice.

Mike, Phil, and Cruz are already deep in conversation. With Halloween right around the corner, Phil can't and won't waste a moment of planning time.

"Hey, buddy," says Mike. "Nice of you to show up."

Mooch plops down next to him and sighs out loud, signaling he's distraught about something. He then shovels another handful of Doritos into his mouth and speedily crunches and swallows. "Guys. I, um . . . I have some bad news."

Sensing that Mooch is troubled by something serious, Mike's facial expression quickly changes from jovial to concerned as Phil and Cruz abruptly stop their conversation.

"Okay, what's up?" asks Mike.

"So . . . I, uh . . . I, um . . . We're," he says in a wobbly voice. "My mom just told me we're moving at the beginning of next year. Right after New Year's."

As Mooch drops his head in sadness, the others remain silent, taking a moment to comprehend this bombshell.

"What?!" shouts Phil, emphatically shoving his glasses up his nose.

"Holy moly!" exclaims Mike.

"Heavy," murmurs Cruz.

"Yeah, I know. I can't believe it," responds Mooch, still staring down at the floor. "So, I guess Halloween 1988 will be my last with you guys."

They collectively contemplate the implications of this news for a few moments before Mike, in an effort to positively change the mood and refocus the gang, blurts, "Then we need to make double sure this is the absolutely best Halloween ever! The Mooch Farewell, Josh Revenge Grand Master Tour! Time to get to work, boys."

Phil shakes his head decisively. He pulls last year's TOTR map from his backpack and carefully unrolls it on the drafting table.

"Hey, Mike, can I come in?" peeps a voice from just outside the clubhouse door. It's Pip, short for Pip-Squeak, the nickname for Mike's younger brother Matt. At nine years old, Pip is in the fourth grade, and for years he's wanted desperately to be a part of Mike's Gang.

"No. Only gang members allowed. Now go, we're busy," replies Mike.

Pip mopes away as the gang members form a huddle around the drafting table and focus on the TOTR map. They begin discussing the first item on their agenda, the most critical aspect of this year's plan: revenge for Josh's Crew stealing their stashed candy last year.

Mooch suggests they develop a master plan to steal all Josh's Crew's candy and then force them to watch as the gang eats it all in front of them. Mike and Phil shoot Mooch a puzzled look that telegraphs *really*, knowing it is virtually impossible to *force* Josh into doing anything.

Mike suggests they be more realistic about their revenge expectations.

Cruz thinks they should simply walk right up to Josh and his cronies, take their candy bags, and walk away with no discussion.

Mike and Phil laugh out loud, knowing Cruz would actually try this, but also knowing Josh would never let such a thing happen. It would quickly turn into a barn burner of a brawl!

Steering the ideas in a more sensible direction, Mike interrupts. "I'm sure we can come up with something better than that. Something we can actually accomplish."

"Yeah, definitely," Phil concurs. "Give me some time. I'll think of something."

They all agree, trusting fully in Phil's planning expertise.

The second, and also highly critical item on their agenda: the lingering, unanswered question of how Josh's Crew knew where the gang had stashed their candy. The gang had put a lot of thought into the stash location and they were very careful not to be seen while stashing it. But somehow Josh and his goons found out and stole their precious loot. The gang cannot risk this scenario happening again this year. Unfortunately, the answer to this question is less mysterious than they may want to admit. Although he's never said anything, and the others have never pushed this delicate topic, the common belief is that Mooch was most likely bamboozled by Terry McDowell into divulging the stash location.

Terry McDowell is a good friend of Lisa Heatherman. Lisa, Veronica (who goes by Roni) Martinez, and Terry are a group of friends in the same grade as Mike's Gang and Josh's Crew, and the groups frequently interact with each other. While Lisa and Roni tend to favor Mike's Gang, Terry tries to maintain a neutral stance but typically leans toward Josh's Crew and enjoys extracting information from Mooch that she can share with Josh.

Mooch has a well-known soft spot, a *very* soft spot, for Terry, and she uses this to her advantage in manipulating him for her own gain. He's always been uncontrollably and embarrassingly susceptible to her trickery. The others know this and as such, typically go easy on him about it. Recognizing that pressing Mooch on this issue will most likely result in a huge argument that will resolve nothing, the gang instead hopes the heightened necessity of achieving success this year will deter Mooch from divulging any sensitive information and quickly end this part of the discussion.

In addition to letting their loot be stolen, Mike's Gang knows other mistakes were made last year. The third item on this evening's agenda stands almost equal in importance to redeeming themselves for last year's debacle: the realization that they spent too much time at the Hotters' house last year. Time must be allotted for the sacred tradition of gazing upon Mrs. Hotter—something every boy in the neighborhood enjoys. However, they all admit the duration spent there should have been shorter to allow more time for other important stops.

Phil, in a brief moment of confusion, suggests perhaps they skip the Hotters' house, given how much they have to accomplish this year. The others immediately dispute this unwelcome suggestion. After taking some time to reminisce about that wondrous stop last year, Phil quickly backs off his statement. They then vehemently agree that skipping the Hotters' house can *never, ever* be an option, but concede that the time spent there this year must be well timed and short—a time limit *must* be established and strictly followed.

The undesired result of lingering too long at the Hotters' house last year was not getting to Cherry Grove early enough. Cherry Grove is the neighborhood south of theirs, down Orchard Street. It's a smaller neighborhood with larger and nicer houses known for handing out awesome candy. It's as if the neighbors there compete to hand out the best and biggest candy, and it gets better with each passing year. It's a trick-or-treating wonderland! The only catch is that the number of trick-or-treaters is high, quickly consuming the supply, so getting there as early as possible is key. Last year the gang managed to hit most houses still offering the best and biggest candy—a.k.a. Candies from the Gods—but missed out at a couple of houses that ran out before they arrived.

While limiting their time at the Hotters' will facilitate getting to Cherry Grove sooner, they fear it still may not be soon enough, considering all they must accomplish first. Looking for other ways to cut time, they inevitably confront the harsh reality that if they're to hit all the good houses in their neighborhood (including the Hotters') and then make it to Cherry Grove in time, they must consider the previously unthinkable. They must confront their fears and pass through the Clarks' yard. Since it's the only way to cut enough time to make it all work, they all agree. With the hair on their heads, necks, and arms now standing due to this monumental commitment, they take a collective deep breath in an attempt to calm themselves.

Pip appears again at the door to the clubhouse, startling the gang. He has two handfuls of Reese's Peanut Butter Cups, smuggled from the kitchen cupboard. Offering the candy as a bribe, he asks again if he can join the meeting. While Mike, Phil, and Cruz take a moment to decide, Mooch quickly rises to snag a couple packages from Pip's hand and immediately begins to unwrap and devour them. Thinking they'd better take their opportunity now before he goes in for seconds, the others grab one each and unwrap and eat them.

"Okay, you can stay. But you have to just sit and listen. No Pip-Squeak questions, comments, ideas, etc., allowed. And, NOT A SINGLE SOLITARY WORD OF WHAT YOU HEAR IS TO BE REPEATED TO ANYONE ELSE. EVER! Okay?" states Mike.

Pip excitedly nods. Mike makes him raise his right hand and swear to the Candy Gods that he'll comply, and Mooch demands he fork over the remaining Reese's Peanut Butter Cups.

Back to work. The gang, Pip now included, huddle again at the clubhouse drafting table. Pointing to spots on last year's TOTR map, Phil begins to offer his suggestions on potential variations to this year's route. He uses a pencil to sketch in new ideas he's been contemplating. Mike and Mooch (in between shoveling handfuls of Doritos into his mouth) add suggestions, as Cruz and Pip listen intently. Phil also conveys his initial thoughts on locations for stashing their loot halfway through the route. Gaining no consensus on a location—or even if stashing candy should be part of this year's plan, given the shock of what happened a year ago—the conversation slowly migrates back to how agonizing it is that Josh was able to get the best of them. These are demons that won't be exorcised until they achieve redemption.

"Dinnertime, boys!" yells Mike's mom through the opened sliding-glass door to the kitchen.

"Time to wrap it up, guys," says Mike as the rest of them groan in disappointment.

They plod out of the clubhouse and into the house.

As they say their good-byes, Mrs. Hendricks asks if they're trick-or-treating with Josh Pealy this year. "He's such a nice boy. You should ask him to go with you."

They all shoot her looks of bewilderment. This sentiment is common among parents in the neighborhood, so they're not surprised. Josh is an expert at deceiving parents, particularly moms, and teachers into thinking he's a good, honest, and upstanding young man. But the neighborhood kids know him for what he truly is—a mean and nasty bully. It drives them absolutely crazy how Josh has been able to get away with manipulating parents and teachers for so long. How can the adults not see what's really going on? How has Josh avoided being discovered?

Knowing he won't convince his mom that Josh isn't the "nice young man" she thinks he is, Mike politely replies, "No, Mom. Just our gang, like always."

After the others leave Mike sits down to dinner and his thoughts revert back to the situation with Lisa, now compounded by Mooch's big news. If he doesn't tell Lisa he isn't going trick-or-treating with her, what he just said may not happen. This is the last year the gang will all be together, so he has to cancel his plans with her. Mooch's bombshell about moving away is just the excuse he needs.

Meanwhile, the girls have gathered in Lisa's bedroom to commence their own trick-or-treating planning.

"Look, I've started my Wonder Woman costume. Coming along very nicely, if I do say so myself," states Lisa proudly as she shows her friends her work.

"Wow! Mike will be amazed! You'll have to pick his chin up off the floor!" exclaims Roni with a laugh.

"And clean his drool off the floor too. He won't be ready for this!" adds Terry in awe of what Lisa has assembled. "Or all the other guys trick-or-treating."

Lisa is considered the prettiest girl in the seventh grade by many. Wearing this Wonder Woman costume will certainly convince any doubters. Terry, who's a more outdoorsy type with a dark, sarcastic nature, isn't altogether fond of Lisa and Roni's shared affinity for clothing, jewelry, perfume, and everything else Terry considers *too girly*. She prefers to maintain a more neutral appearance with her lazily styled short, sandy-blond, semi-curly hair and more practical apparel. But she forces herself to engage as much as she can in her friends' conversations about style because she enjoys their fun-loving banter and wit. Lisa and Roni are aware of Terry's disdain for fashion, but they suspect she likes it more than she lets on. Above all, they admire and enjoy the consistent comedic value she offers, particularly when talking to boys. But, it's Terry's uncontrollable desire for devious behavior that the other two don't approve of—which creates conflict within Mike's Gang on occasion.

Roni, for all intents and purposes, is Lisa's best friend, her sidekick. She shares Lisa's interests, is always there for her, and she's also one of the most attractive girls in the seventh grade. Roni and Lisa are always together, always enjoy each other's company, and always dress fashionably. Roni's medium-length straight black hair is a stark contrast to Lisa's long, wavy light-brown hair, but it's elegant in its own way. She is kindhearted, but very protective of her friends. She'll stop at nothing to defend them.

Lisa is well-behaved, intelligent, and articulate. She dreams of having a career in business. Her love for fashion is equaled by her love for getting excellent grades, and she dedicates many hours to studying to ensure her success. In addition to her intimidatingly good looks, her sharp wit is often a deterrent to any unworthy would-be suitors. By all accounts, Lisa is very well rounded.

"Yeah," Lisa replies to Terry, "I want it to be amazing! You know how into costumes Mike and his friends are. My costume has to be perfect to compete with his," she continues. "I bought this Wonder Woman comic book to make sure I get her outfit right. I want this to be the most memorable night ever for Mike."

"Oh, I'm pretty sure it will be," replies Terry.

"You think? I hope so. I don't know, maybe I need more sparkle? You think I need more sparkle? Brighter colors too?" continues Lisa. "It's all I can think about ever since Mike agreed to go trick-or-treating with me. I'm so excited I can hardly stand it!"

"From what you've put together so far, it's going to be amazing," says Roni. "Mike will be impressed, for sure."

"Thanks! I sure hope so. I can't seem to find a lasso, though. Any ideas?"

"Isn't Wonder Women's lasso invisible?" asks Terry.

"No, I don't think so. I think her helicopter—no, her plane—is?" replies Roni.

"Yeah, her plane is, according to the comic books," Lisa verifies.

"Oh. Well, why not just take a string and paint it gold or something?" inquires Terry.

"Paint? Paint?! I can't buy a rope and paint it. My dad could, but he's out of town on business until Halloween. I'll just see if my mom has something that will work," states Lisa. "How are your costumes coming along?"

"Well, mine is easy since my mom was a cheerleader at Texas Christian University—she still has her uniform. The TCU cheerleader outfits are very similar to the ones the Dallas Cowboys' cheerleaders wear," replies Roni. "I just have to find some white boots. Does your mom have any that I could borrow?"

"We can look," Lisa replies.

"I haven't even thought about my costume yet. Maybe I'll go as Joan Jett," adds Terry. "We'll see."

"Cool!" replies Lisa distractedly. "I can't wait to see Mike in his Superman costume. I can't think of a more fitting costume for him," she says as she tightly hugs the pillow she's just grabbed off her bed.

"Well, I don't know if I agree with that," replies Terry as she makes a gagging expression while inserting her finger into her mouth. As always, Terry outwardly projects the sentiment that she's not fond of boys—any boys, at all, ever. However, they're beginning to grow on her, and that change of heart is starting to trickle out more and more—something her friends are aware of and tease her about, but only sparingly because they know how sensitive she can be.

"What? Is it better suited for *Josh*?" replies Roni as she bats her eyelashes exaggeratedly at Terry.

"No! That's not what I was say—"

"Uh-huh," replies an unconvinced Roni, who turns her focus back to Lisa. "Well, you two will make an *incredibly, amazingly* wonderful couple parading *magnificently* around Cherry Grove." She pauses. "I wonder what costume Cruz will be wearing?"

"Who cares?" retorts Terry.

"Oh! I wish Halloween were tomorrow!" exclaims Lisa.

With an eye roll to convey her disgust, Terry replies, "Yeah, it's going to be a momentous occasion."

After glaring at Terry for an extended moment, Lisa continues, "Okay. Let's go see what we can find in my mom's closet."

"Yeah! Hopefully some knee-high white boots!" adds Roni.

"Yay," murmurs Terry sarcastically as she follows slowly behind the other two.

5

Map Leak

Terry knows Mooch has a crush on her (something his friends *cannot* understand given the condescending manner in which she constantly treats him) and she often uses this to her advantage. Typically, she enjoys just toying with him in good fun, but on occasion she relishes the added benefit of extracting valuable information to share with Josh. Having her own crush on Josh, she shares this information freely, hoping to impress him and, thus, get him to pay attention to her. Accordingly, Josh is always eager to gain any and all information that potentially gives him an advantage over others, especially Mike and his gang. Aware of Terry's crush and that she's constantly on the lookout for any nugget of valuable information, Josh considers her his "undercover secret agent" and sometimes calls her the "fifth member" of his crew.

Terry's motives are obvious to Mike, Phil, and Cruz and it angers them very much. Mooch is also aware of the disingenuous nature of her supposed "kindness" toward him but he's trapped by his uncontrollable attraction to her. His friends have been forced, repeatedly, to witness disgusting interactions between himself and Terry, either firsthand or via stories from others. For the life of them, they cannot figure this out: How in the heck can Mooch be so goo-goo over her? How in the heck can he be so gullible as to fall for her transparently manipulative tactics time and again? Nonetheless, there's little they can do to stop it, other than protecting Mooch from himself as much as possible by intervening every chance they get. Problem is, they can't be there every time.

"Hey, Smooch, are you trick-or-treating with your boys this year?" asks Terry as she approaches Mooch, who's haphazardly gathering items from his disorganized half-height locker located in the upper tier.

Excited that Terry is talking to him and eager to impress her, Mooch replies, "Yes! Of course, it's our favorite thing—we love it—should be a world record year . . . Are you going with Lisa and Roni?"

"Haven't decided yet. I may go with them or maybe go with Josh and his crew. Don't know. We'll see," she replies, trying to play it cool.

"Pealy," Mooch murmurs under his breath. "Hmm . . . Okay . . . Well, our gang always sticks together, we always stick to our route—follow our map."

As the last words of this sentence escape his mouth, a wave of panic washes over him, realizing he's just let it slip that they have a trick-or-treating map. Something they've always kept a secret, something they've all solemnly vowed to never divulge, ever. Trying to think on his feet, something he isn't particularly adept at, he quickly tries to change the subject. "The weather should be nice—"

"Map?" replies Terry inquisitively, her interest now piqued.

"Uh . . . What? Map? Did I say *map*?" he nervously replies, beginning to sweat, as he mentally yells at himself: *Stop saying the word* map! "I, uh . . . I meant . . . We . . . We just like to, uh . . . We just have a path we like to stick to. *Map* is just a figure of speech."

Sensing she's begun to extract a significant piece of information that Josh will certainly want, she jumps on the opportunity to goad him into divulging more. Completely ignoring Mooch's feeble and downright pathetic attempt to dampen her curiosity, she responds in her typical demeaning tone, "What kind of *map* do you have? Is it like a *treasure* map?"

Mooch knows he's messed up, big time. He's divulged something he shouldn't have, something his friends wouldn't be happy about, and it could be disastrous. Just revealing this information to an outsider is in and of itself a BIG mistake, but spilling it to Terry makes it the most GIGANTIC, HUMUNGOUS, MEGA mistake of all time! If he can't wiggle out of this predicament and convince her there's not really a map, and if she passes this information on to Josh, it will be catastrophic. Josh can't find out he and his friends have a map! He'll surely use all his evil talents to obtain it—a circumstance Mooch *cannot* let play out.

"Treasure map, ha! I wish . . . A treasure map to the chest of endless candy! Wouldn't that be something. If only it were true," he states, desperately grasping for any words that might distract Terry.

Now completely focused on her objective, she presses, "Where is this map? Do you have it with you now? Can I take a peek at it? Just a small peek? It sounds amazing, Smooch."

"Ha! Sure, if I had one, I'd show it to you. But there is NO map. Just a route we pick and follow in our heads—you know, from memory," he replies in the most convincing voice he can muster.

"Oh, come on, Smoochy, let me see the—"

"What's going on there?" asks Mike from down the hallway.

Mooch, as is typical when talking to any girl, particularly Terry, is embarrassed and red-faced, speaking in haphazard and incoherent fragments, profusely sweating, and breathing rapidly.

Terry looks as she has so many times while speaking to Mooch—like she's up to no good and enjoying every second of it.

As he closes the distance, Mike senses Mooch is being manipulated yet again and knows he must stop this conversation before Mooch potentially divulges sensitive information, assuming he hasn't already. "Everything okay?!"

Knowing that's all the information she's going to get from Mooch for now, Terry abruptly makes her escape, bolting just before Mike reaches them. As she strolls away with her back to the boys, she waves one arm over her head in a bye-bye motion.

"Hey," says Mike, looking at Mooch inquisitively.

"Hey," replies Mooch, shifting his eyes from the departing Terry to the floor in front of him.

"So, what did she want?"

"Oh . . . uh, she just wanted to know something about some homework we have due in science class."

"That's it? Looked like she was pressing you pretty hard about something," replies Mike, not entirely believing Mooch's response.

"Yes! That's it. It was nothing. No big deal. She wasn't pressing me."

Strongly suspecting something has gone awry, Mike contemplates digging deeper. After thinking it over for a couple of seconds, he decides not to pursue it further because he doesn't want to put Mooch on the spot and potentially embarrass him. He's also not sure he actually wants to know what he and Terry were talking about.

Mooch's tone abruptly changes to fear as he begins to tell Mike about the terrible nightmare he had last night. "Oh, man! Had the scariest nightmare last night! Josh was at every house we trick-or-treated. At every doorbell we rang, he'd open the door and say, 'I've got some fresh, shiny pennies for you boys. Ha!' as he showed us old brownish-greenish ones. But then he'd hand out homemade hard peppermint candies. Ugh, peppermint—the thought of it is . . . Anyway, after a while we decided to try a piece, since this was the only type of candy we kept getting all night. When I bit into mine, my front teeth cracked—all four in front! They all split into pieces and fell out of my mouth, scattering all over the floor! Left a huge hole, ruining my perfect smile. Then you guys disappeared and Josh reappears out of nowhere . . . *POOF* . . . and starts laughing at me with the entire school behind him laughing at me too. It was awful!"

"Wow! That does sound bad."

"Yeah. Josh had *that* look on his face. You know, the one he's always giving us like he's just sabotaged something or planned a surprise attack. Like he knows something we don't, like he's better than us? I hate that look . . . Only, in the nightmare he had these bright-orange, glowing eyes and sharp black horns, like small bull horns, coming out of the top of his head. Was so scary."

"So, they weren't his everyday horns?" jokes Mike.

"Ha! Yeah . . . No, these were new ones, bigger and scarier ones," replies Mooch laughing, momentarily sidetracked from his story. "It got even worse though. Seeing my broken teeth, my mom banned me from eating *all* candy for the *rest* of my life, even chocolate! She said it was 'for my own good' and that I couldn't 'risk breaking any more teeth eating candy.' It was so depressing."

"That would be awful."

"I tried to argue with her, but Josh suddenly appeared next to her, *poof*, and lectured me alongside her. I had to argue with both of them! Oh my god, it was terrible. Pealy was everywhere, making my life MISERABLE. I finally woke up, soaked in sweat with my heart pounding out of my chest . . . You think that could really happen, Mikey?"

"What? That you could break your teeth eating candy?"

"All of it. The whole nightmare. Josh, my teeth, my mom?!"

"I highly doubt it," answers Mike reassuringly, as Phil and Cruz walk up to them.

Mooch looks down to the floor in front of him worriedly, not convinced by Mike's response. Phil and Cruz say hi and ask what they're talking about. Mike quickly paraphrases Mooch's nightmare for them. The three of them laugh out loud and then collectively yell "Pealy!" mimicking Mooch's go-to cry of frustration. Realizing how ridiculous the nightmare story sounds now, hearing Mike retell it, Mooch manages a chuckle as his anxiety subsides.

"Smoochy, Smoochy, Smoochy. You scaredy scared?" says Phil mimicking Terry with his lips puckered, acting as though he's going to kiss Mooch.

"Shut up!" replies Mooch, annoyed.

Phil continues, trying to get him riled up, "Oh, Smoochy, Sm—"

"That's enough," interrupts Mike as he covers Phil's mouth with his hand.

With Cruz also giving him a stern look of displeasure—the look that says "You better stop it or I'll stop it for you," Phil quickly complies. Mooch continues to angrily stare down Phil for a second or two, but he's interrupted by the ring of the bell, signaling it's time for their next class.

As they walk away, Mooch's thoughts swirl while he anguishes over divulging the valuable information to Terry. He tries to convince himself that she'll forget about it and that he and his buddies have nothing to worry about. But deep down he knows Terry won't forget. She'll leak the information to Josh, leaving them vulnerable to another attack from his crew.

Mike wonders what Mooch has said to Terry and what it means for the gang. Did he reveal crucial information that could come back to haunt them, or was Terry just toying with Mooch for fun?

Phil ponders if Mooch's nightmare is some sort of Halloween premonition that could somehow come true. He tries to shrug off this notion. As long as he develops a rock-solid plan and he and the rest of the gang execute it like only they can, everything will work out just fine.

6

Rookie Gang

Jimmy Krisyzniak is the ten-year-old leader of a group Mooch has dubbed the Rookie Gang. Every year these rookies attempt to emulate the trick-or-treating expertise of their idols, Mike's Gang. Like them, they love everything about Halloween and strive to gather as much of the best candy as they can. While flattered by their admiration, Mike's Gang is equally annoyed by their constant pestering to divulge their trick-or-treating ideas, techniques, procedures, etc.—a cumbersome routine that begins in early October and continues until November 1 every year.

Finished with their lunch, Jimmy and the other Rookie Gang members, Beau (goes by Buck) Thompson and the identical twins Jake and Nick Brooks, head outside to the playground. As is typical, these fifth graders are headed straight for the basketball court—where they know Mike's Gang will be.

"Hey, Mooch!" yells Jimmy, walking briskly along the playground's dark-gray asphalt pavement toward Mooch and Mike, who are busy searching for an acceptable basketball out of the metal-screened bin of sports equipment that was just rolled outside by the playground monitor.

"Oh, no. Here they come," says Mooch under his breath as Mike lets out a long sigh of disappointment.

"Ready for Halloween, guys?!" asks Jimmy.

Mike and Mooch stand motionless and silent for a couple of seconds, staring at Jimmy, wondering what nagging questions are soon to follow and how much time he'll steal from their lives today.

"Ha! Of course you are. What am I thinking?" continues Jimmy nervously. "Are your costumes this year going to be as awesome as they were last year? *Top Gun, The Untouchables*—classic!"

Mike and Mooch remain silent. A response will only lead to more annoying questions they'd rather not hear. Hopefully, by some miracle, Jimmy will give up on this one-way conversation and go away.

"You guys have a great route planned for this year? Going to get mega amounts of candy? I wish we could pull off trick-or-treating like you guys," continues Jimmy as the Brooks twins walk up behind him. "How about sharing some of your trick-or-treating secrets with us? Please, just one. Maybe an old trick you don't use anymore to help us out?"

With the Brooks twins' interest now piqued, Jake chimes in, "Yeah, one super-awesome trick would be great!"

"One day we *may* decide to divulge *some* of our secrets to you wannabe-expert trick-or-treaters, but that day isn't today," retorts Mooch, having had enough already. "And not any day this year either. Maybe when we retire, when we finally decide to hang up our bags . . . Or maybe never," he continues.

Mike laughs.

"Come on. Just one secret, guys?!" pleads Nick.

"Look, no information is going to be revealed—not on my watch! And now it's time for you knuckleheads to stop wasting our time and buzz off—we've got a basketball game to play!" exclaims Mooch, his aggravation growing having to deal with questions from all three now.

Mike just chuckles again, refusing to get involved in a never-ending conversation with these rookies. But he enjoys watching yet another hilarious and pointless episode of Mooch versus Jimmy and company.

Dejected, Jimmy turns to walk away. After a single step his frustration gets the best of him, and he abruptly turns back to Mooch to launch a verbal parting shot, "I've got a secret for you, Pooch—if you didn't spend all day every day eating, you wouldn't be so fat!"

Turning back around to continue walking away, Jimmy takes one step and is startled to find himself looking directly into Cruz's chest. He tilts his head up and sees Cruz's eyes staring back at him intimidatingly. Cruz heard every awful word Jimmy just said and isn't happy about it one bit.

Stopping dead in his tracks, terrified, Jimmy can only mutter, "Uh . . ."

Cruz, still peering down at him, pushes his chest further into Jimmy's face.

"Sorry, Brooz—I mean, Mr. Brooz," sputters Jimmy, looking up at him apologetically. He slowly turns to face Mooch again. "I was only kidding, You know, just playing around."

After waiting a few seconds for Brooz to make a move, Jimmy realizes he's not going to. Very slowly and very carefully, Jimmy sidesteps him, walks a few more paces, and then runs speedily away toward the red-brick school building.

Mike, watching the entire episode, continues to chuckle while Mooch laughingly yells, "You better run! Rookie!"

The Brooks twins choose not to run away with Jimmy and instead courageously (or more appropriately, *stupidly*) decide to continue the questioning, figuring Cruz won't hear them, being preoccupied with Jimmy.

"How many tons of candy did you eat last year before, during, and after trick-or-treating?" asks Jake as Nick smiles alongside him.

Choosing to ignore the condescending tone of this remark, Mooch instead takes the opportunity to boast, "Well, it was a truly amazing spectacle, boys! The most masterful exhibition of chocolate consumption the world has ever seen, or may never see again. Worthy of an audience by the greatest candy makers of all time—the likes of Willy Wonka or Sir Hershey himself!"

Jake and Nick, appreciating this masterfully creative and exuberant response, laugh loudly.

Nick then admits, "We attempted to eat our entire loot too. Bad idea. Ended up getting sick and then grounded by our mom."

"Shameful! Rookies!" replies Mooch jokingly as he and Mike chuckle.

Hearing the friendly banter from a distance and feeling left out, Jimmy bravely decides to return to the group, hoping to join in the laughter.

Regaining his confidence, he asks, "So, you guys want to trick-or-treat together this year? It would be fun!"

"Nope," retorts Mooch as Mike simultaneously replies, "Not happening."

"You guys make too many mistakes," continues Mooch as Mike again simultaneously replies, "Can't risk it."

Commencing a final attempt at persuading them, Jimmy starts, "Come on—"

Phil, who's just joined the group, feels compelled to interject. "Look, you guys don't put in the hard work it takes to achieve success. We do. We can't afford to risk our success by taking a chance with you lame-os slowing us down or doing something stupid."

"Well, if you shared your tricks with us, we wouldn't—"

"Not happening," Mooch interrupts. "Our techniques are way too elaborate for inexperienced hacks like you," says Mooch.

"Don't take it personal, guys. We don't trick-or-treat with anyone. The four of us only go with each other. Every year. Always," adds Phil.

"Remember when you guys made that MAJOR mistake last year? You know, when you got sloppy and went to the Anchors' house with Josh's Crew following right behind you," recalls Mooch.

Continuing the story, Phil says, "Yeah, the Anchors' house?! The house with the best candy in the neighborhood! With Josh and his goons stalking you, ready to pounce and take the candy from you? Which is exactly what happened. A costly, careless, and shameful move. A *rookie* move."

Knowing the story is true and having no countering response, Jimmy and the twins just stand there, silently embarrassed.

"You have to be more careful. You have to plan better. You have to be on your toes at all times. You never know when, where, or how Josh will pounce," explains Mike, thinking this suggestion needs to be taken to heart by his gang as well.

Relishing the opportunity to pile on, Mooch recalls how these guys always get to the please-take-just-one house too late as well. "Ha! You guys also always make it to the Gully—"

Not wanting Mooch to assist these guys any more in their planning for this year's trick-or-treating, Phil cuts him off by coughing loudly and quickly changes the subject. "Okay, that's enough, we have more important things to do than continue with this nonsense."

"Well, I guess we'll just ask Josh and his crew for help," retorts Jimmy, trying to mask his frustration.

"Good luck with that," replies Mike, shaking his head in disbelief. "That's a good way to get ALL your candy taken."

Now feeling the need to assist them from making a grave mistake, Phil advises, "For your own safety, I must caution you, that is highly NOT recommended. You will cross into very dangerous territory if you go down that road."

Seething again over what happened to them last year at the hands of Josh, Mooch murmurs, "Pealy . . ."

Feeling somewhat sorry for them, Mike gives the Rookie Gang some parting advice, "Look, guys, you just have to be smarter this year. Start with keeping track of Pealy and his goons, and then try to stay ahead of them. Move as quickly as you can."

Wanting to get a little basketball in before their next class, the gang abruptly turns and starts walking away. As they go, they discuss how they should also be implementing the advice Mike's just given to the Rookie Gang. They must be on their toes at all times. They must be one step ahead of Josh's Crew or risk a similar—or perhaps even worse—fate this year. At least their expert trick-or-treating reputations are safe. Only they and Josh's Crew know what went down last year. They have Josh's desire to keep his misdeeds quiet to thank for that. Still, the gang is determined to take every possible step necessary to ensure last year's humiliation isn't repeated this year.

7

Lisa and Mike
Not ~Trick-Or-Treating?

As they walk to school the gang engages in their typical banter about various topics ranging from baseball to movies to Halloween costumes to video games to favorite candies to the TOTR. With Halloween nearly here, their excitement is high and the laughs are coming more often and louder than usual. At least for everyone except Mike.

He's distracted. He knows he *must* tell Lisa he can't trick-or-treat with her and he knows he *must* do it soon. He feels so bad about having to go back on his promise to her, but with the news of Mooch's eminent departure, he has no choice—this will be his gang's last hurrah together—he has to go with his buddies. He has to tell her today, before it gets too close to Halloween. He decides to tell her during homeroom, the first period of the day. That's his best chance to break the news with none of his, or her, friends around. It should be the ideal setting to have a private conversation, in a public place, which should lower the chance of inciting an ugly scene.

The other gang members notice Mike isn't himself this morning and ask what's wrong a couple of times along the way. But Mike just shrugs off these questions. "I'm just tired. Didn't sleep well last night." An accurate statement, as Mike was awake for much of the night contemplating his next move with Lisa.

As the others debate various random topics and poke fun at one another, Mike can't stop daydreaming—or more appropriately, day-night-

45

maring—about how mad, really mad, Lisa is going to be. He envisions her hearing the news and screaming at the top of her lungs while throwing objects and slapping, or perhaps punching, him in the face in front of the entire homeroom. This will be followed by her storming out of the classroom and slamming the door behind her, leaving only the proverbial solitary sound of crickets chirping in her wake.

Not wanting to face such a dreadful fate, Mike attempts to dismiss it by murmuring to himself, "She wouldn't. She'll understand. She'll be fine with it . . ."

"What?" replies Phil as the three of them stare at Mike, Mooch abruptly stopping the candy story he's currently in the middle of.

"Huh?" Mike replies. "Oh. Uh, nothing. Just thinking about something that happened at home this morning."

Not believing his response, but not concerned enough to press further, the others shoot him puzzled looks for a second or two and then reengage in Mooch's story.

As he approaches the school, Mike becomes more nervous with each step. After walking up the steps and entering through the brown painted-metal entry doors, Mike says good-bye to his pals with uncharacteristic hurriedness. As he makes his way down the hall, each step is slower than the last. He's nearly at a standstill by the time he approaches his homeroom. Frozen in place, staring at the doorway, he finds it difficult to talk himself into passing through, dreading what's surely to come—the thought of turning and running crosses his mind at least once. Now feeling nauseous and noticeably sweating, Mike walks in and sits in his assigned seat, right behind Lisa, who is already seated and turned sideways in her chair, gazing at his every move.

"Hey there!" she says, smiling and excited. "You okay?" Her tone turns from jovial to concerned.

"Huh? Oh, yeah. I'm okay, just not feeling 100 percent this morning," he replies timidly.

The bell rings and Lisa turns forward to face the teacher at the front of the classroom. Her long brown hair swings around and partially lands on Mike's desktop. Completely oblivious to everything the teacher is saying, he marvels at how perfectly arranged her hair is. Taking in the scent of her perfume, or lotion, or whatever is making her smell so good, he thinks that maybe he should just go trick-or-treating with her as he agreed. The guys will understand—look at her, she looks amazing! Shaking his head forcefully side to side to snap out of this Lisa trance, he realizes that wouldn't go over well with the guys, at all—not an option.

His attention turns back to pondering the impending doom he expects to experience soon. His mind starts an agonizing race through multiple scenarios of how he'll tell Lisa and how she'll respond.

Scenario 1

Mike waits until they're both in the hallway outside of homeroom and then tells Lisa point-blank, "Lisa, I'm really sorry but I just can't go trick-or-treating with you this year. I have to go with my gang."

Lisa screams at the top of her lungs, drawing the attention of everyone in the hallway, "What?! How dare you!"

Mike tries desperately to calm her down by explaining the situation with Mooch in more detail, but she's too upset to listen. She just keeps yelling about how upset and disappointed she is.

Not liking the predicted outcome of this scenario, Mike thinks to himself, *Yikes! No good.*

Scenario 2

To avoid direct confrontation, Mike has Mooch tell Lisa he can't go with her later in the day. But while envisioning this scenario, Mike can't fight off the image of Mooch engulfing a giant candy bar in a very messy fashion, spewing bits of chocolate and saliva toward Lisa, while nonchalantly breaking the news to her.

While Lisa disgustedly picks a chunk of chocolate off of her perfectly appointed top and angrily tosses it to the side, she takes a moment to let what Mooch has just told her sink in and to let the horrific eating spectacle she's just witnessed dissipate from her mind. She looks him sternly in the eyes and yells, "What?! Why?! And, why are *you* telling me this? Where's Mike? I want to talk to *Mike* about this, not *you*. This is none of *your* business."

Mooch then bumbles through an incoherent response for a few seconds until Lisa abruptly stops him, calmly removes the remaining uneaten portion of the chocolate bar from his hand, and proceeds to throw it as far as she can down the hallway. Watching longingly as the candy slides down the hallway, eventually crashing into a locker, Mooch turns back to Lisa with a look of absolute surprise and fear on his face. Lisa then methodically wipes all the chocolate residue from her hand onto Mooch's chest, swiping her hand up and down until clean—staining a good portion of his shirt—and then calmly turns and slowly walks away.

Liking the predicted outcome of *this* scenario even less, Mike thinks, *That's no good either. Can't put my best friend in a dangerous situation like that.*

Scenario 3

Mike waits until lunch and tells her, "Lisa. Hey, uh, I'm sorry, but I just can't let the guys down this year. I *have* to trick-or-treat with them; it's a big year with Mooch moving soon and all. Sorry, but I'm not going to be able to go with you this year."

"What?! Why did you agree to go with me then? I've already started my costume—actually, it's almost finished," she replies. "So, you knew you couldn't go with me when I asked, but told me yes anyway?! Not nice. Not cool. At all."

Mike stammers to explain that he learned about Mooch moving *after* she asked him, but she's in no mood for listening to anything else he has to say. After staring him down for a few moments (seeming like an eternity to Mike) in complete disappointment, Lisa calmly picks up Mike's milk carton from his tray and slowly pours the entire contents of it on top of his head. Mike remains motionless as streams of milk flow down his face and the back of his neck into his shirt and ultimately dripping onto the floor.

Liking the predicted outcome of this scenario the least, Mike aggravatingly shakes his head again and thinks, *Ugh. There are no good options for this.*

His attention now returned to the present, mentally fatigued from thinking through the scenarios, he retreats back to the serenity of gazing upon Lisa's beautiful hair and vaguely listening to the announcements being broadcast over the classroom speaker.

As the end of the class nears, his level of anxiety reaches DEFCON 1. He drifts off again, thinking to himself that maybe he should just wait until the day of Halloween and then tell Lisa he's sick and can't go. But then he'd be letting his gang down, ruining all their plans, getting no Halloween candy . . . Maybe he could just tell Lisa he's sick, but then sneak out with his buddies and make sure he doesn't see her on the route. He's good at planning. He could pull this off, right? No way. She'd definitely track him down or at the very least, someone else would see him and tell her he was out—way too many ways for that plan to go bad. Maybe he can blame it on his little brother Pip and say his mom is making Mike bring him and his friends along. That might actually work since Pip can be annoying (especially to girls), a situation Lisa would likely not want to deal with. But then he and his gang would be stuck trick-or-treating with Pip and his completely annoying friends for the entire night, which would surely compromise their plans. Not to mention the other difficulties of that scenario, like convincing his gang to allow Pip's group to tag along, dealing with Pip's group slowing them down, not wanting Pip's group to undeservingly benefit from the fruits of their masterful plan, and experiencing the awkwardness when they eventually run into Lisa and she divulges how Mike backed out on going with her this year. No good. Too many negatives—not worth the risk.

Mentally exhausted from running through the potential excuses, Mike once and for all acknowledges to himself that he can't lie to Lisa and decides he must tell her the truth, straight up.

As the bell signaling the end of homeroom rings, Mike follows Lisa through the door. She stops into the hallway just outside the classroom and turns to smile widely at Mike. Shaking slightly from nervousness and sweating profusely, Mike sheepishly begins to speak.

"Lisa."

"Yes, Mike," she replies as she gazes at him.

"I, uh . . . I . . . I just can't go trick-or-treating with you this year. It's Mooch's last Halloween here—he's moving away early next year—and so, being our last Halloween together, we made a pact to make this our best trick-or-treating year ever . . . I'm really sorry, but I can't let the guys down. I can't let Mooch down," he explains and starts raising his hands to cover his face, a preemptive reactionary move to shield himself from her anticipated rage.

Masking her disappointment, Lisa remains emotionless, playing it cool. "Oh . . . okay. No big deal. I understand . . . You should go with your boys."

Mike drops his hands to his sides and stares at Lisa speechless, completely taken off-guard by her response. After a couple of silent and awkward seconds, he finally comes out of shock and replies, "Okay . . . Well, I'm sure I'll see you out there."

"Yeah. I'm sure you will, Michael," she replies stoically as Roni walks up from behind and stands next to her, looking over the duo inquisitively.

With nothing left to discuss, Mike politely says good-bye to both of them and turns around to move down the hall to his next class. As he walks away, he finds himself relieved that she didn't explode, yet disappointed he won't be going with her. Recounting the conversation, he becomes consumed with wondering why she called him Michael. "That can't be good, can it?" he mumbles under his breath. "I don't think she's ever called me Michael."

After a moment of watching Mike walk away, Roni turns to Lisa and notices the look of sadness on her face. "What just happened?"

"He just cancelled on me. We're not trick-or-treating together this year," responds Lisa as she gazes longingly upon Mike disappearing down the hallway.

"What?! Why?"

"Basically, he'd rather go with his gang than with me." Lisa doesn't mention (due to not hearing it, being preoccupied by the shock of what Mike was saying) that it will be Mooch's last Halloween here.

"That's not cool. Didn't see that coming."

"Yeah . . . Right? I can't believe he cancelled . . . How dare he . . . He's made a bad decision . . . A decision he's going to regret." Lisa's look of sadness transforms to anger and her gaze at Mike transforms to a glare.

As they walk toward their next class, Roni begins to wonder if this is one of those rare instances when Lisa will seek revenge, if she'll decide Mike must pay for his actions.

8

Planning Meeting 2

Parked on the cool, hard concrete floor of Phil's garage, Mooch is shoveling peanut M&M's into his mouth from the large, yellow, family-size bag sitting on the floor next to him. In a continuous motion, he fluidly transfers the candies from the bag to his mouth, chewing and swallowing them at high speed—a spectacle of perfectly engineered biological conveyance.

Under the constant buzz of the bright fluorescent lighting emanating from the white-painted ceiling, Mike and Phil sit on deteriorating wooden stools with Cruz standing next to them at the workbench located along the back wall—the area the gang have dubbed the workshop.

In front of a backdrop of assorted tools hanging from pegboards secured to the wall, Phil shows off his ergonomic, compartmentalized trick-or-treating bag, a large one made of heavy orange cloth that his mom has modified based on his detailed specifications. It's equipped with a well-padded shoulder strap to make it easier to carry and contains multiple pockets for organized storing of various types of candy. The others—well, at least Mike and Cruz, Mooch is preoccupied at the moment—gaze upon it in awe.

"My mom can make one for each of us," says Phil.

"Yes!" exclaim Mike and Cruz in unison.

Hearing the excitement in their voices, Mooch pauses his M&M's inhalation for a brief moment to look up at the others and give a thumbs-up with a big M&M's-filled smile on his face.

"And my dad is going to waterproof them in case it rains," adds Phil.

Not recalling a year with more than an occasional light drizzle on Halloween, the others don't completely understand the necessity of this, but they shrug it off as Phil being over-prepared as usual.

Then he shows them the sketch he's completed for the candy-storage backpacks he wants to create—expandable to facilitate storage of large quantities of candy and equipped with a bottom compartment to hold ice packs to help prevent the chocolate from melting: "To keep our chocolate cool—it's supposed to be hot again this year. My mom can make these too!"

With his attention now fully captured, Mooch stops eating, lumbers to his feet, gulps down the M&M's remaining in his mouth, and pronounces, "Awesome, Phil! Genius! No melted candy for *us* this year!"

"Yeah, I think keeping our candy stash mobile this year is the safest and most reliable method," replies Phil proudly.

Cruz and Mike agree, but Mooch is unsure. He's focused more on all the weight he'll have to carry around and less about the likeliness of their stash being stolen again.

"Maybe we make carrying *all* our candy around in the backpacks *all* night long our backup plan and try to find a place, a better, more secret place, along the route to stash our loot?" suggests Mooch.

"I don't know about that. You want to give Pealy and his band of thugs an opportunity to steal our stash again?" replies Phil.

"Yeah, I don't think we should take that kind of chance," states Mike as Cruz nods in agreement.

"I'm just saying we should give it some thought. That's all," murmurs Mooch unhappily. "What say should I have, it's just my last Halloween here *ever*."

"Mooch, we can't risk it. We've got to keep all our candy with us at all times this year—Phil's mom is going to make awesome bags that'll make it easier to carry and we'll have cooled backpacks to keep it all fresh. This is definitely safer than stashing it," concludes Mike.

Still troubled at the thought of lugging a heavy load of candy around all night, Mooch desperately tries to come up with another argument to change the others' minds. "How about we stash a wagon halfway through the route, put our first batch of candy in there, and then pull that behind us the rest of the way?"

"No way!" exclaim Mike and Phil together.

"That's the worst possible plan. It would be such easy pickings for Josh and his crew. We may as well just hand our candy over to them on a rolling silver platter," argues Phil.

"Plus, we're going to have to be as nimble as possible if we're going to pass successfully through the Clarks' yard. We can't accomplish that pulling a wagon," adds Mike.

"Yeah, I guess. Not that we'll be all that *nimble* with each of us carrying a huge load around. Maybe this is finally the year for bikes?" offers Mooch.

Every year, something prompts someone to bring up the idea of using bikes and every year they all debate, in great detail, the pros and cons—bikes or no bikes.

As usual, Phil is partially for it, feeling bikes would speed things up for the "standard" (well-known) parts of the route. But he's also partially against it, feeling bikes could hinder them for the "nonstandard" (unknown) parts.

Mike believes repeating the pattern of stopping and dropping the bikes on the driveway, walking to the porch, walking back to the bikes, getting back on, and riding to the next house will cost them time and take more effort than just walking.

Cruz is indifferent on the subject.

Mooch has traditionally been in favor of bikes for Halloween. He agrees with Phil's positive points, but gets conflicted when Mike offers his perspective. Mooch is uncertain as to which method will require the least energy. He likes the idea of using bikes to ease the load of carrying *all* his candy around with him *all* night, figuring he can rest his bags on his bike or add a basket in the back to stash it in. But maybe all the pedaling and dismounting and mounting of the bikes at every house will be too much work.

Phil swiftly kicks into creativity mode and suggests they implement ice-cooled candy storage compartments resting behind the bike seats. He starts thinking out loud how this would work traversing through the Clarks' yard. They could potentially hide the bikes near the Clarks' house and retrieve them later. Realizing this is essentially the same as stashing their loot somewhere along the TOTR, he concludes that taking bikes isn't the way to go.

In attempt to put the issue to bed once and for all, Mike gives a convincing concluding monologue. Bikes make it difficult to maneuver in crowds, can't be brought to porches, must be stashed before entering the Clarks' yard and retrieved after, are susceptible to breaking down (flat tires, dislodged chains, etc.), give more opportunity to Josh's Crew, etc., etc., etc. "Bringing bikes is *not* a good option, at all, guys."

He reminds the others that they still have a lot of work to do in finalizing the route and finishing the plan and strongly suggests they stick to that and not get distracted *again* contemplating bikes. Taking a few moments to digest this compelling argument, the others—including a reluctant Mooch—have no choice but to agree.

Mooch spends a few more moments racking his brain to conjure a last-ditch argument that will convince the others to change their minds, but cannot come up with anything that has a chance of working. Searching desperately for any way to ease his efforts while trick-or-treating, he inquires, "If I put a helium-filled balloon in my bag, you guys think it would make it lighter? Easier to carry?"

Laughing, Phil responds, "Maybe a little, but not enough to make a difference."

"And, the size of the balloon you would need to make a difference would take up most of the room in your bag," adds Mike.

Mooch shrugs in acceptance of defeat. Taking up *any* room in his bag with anything but candy is *not* an option, Mooch sits back down on the floor next to the bag of peanut M&M's and resumes shoveling candy into his mouth. *Well, maybe I could tie the balloon to the outside of my bag and see if that works*, he thinks.

After a short while of preliminary trick-or-treating planning (as is also customary), the conversation shifts to the traditional discussion of costumes.

ACCEPTABLE COSTUMES: superheroes (Superman, Batman, Spiderman, etc.); action-movie characters (*Star Wars*, *Star Trek*, *Crocodile Dundee*, etc.); warriors (knights, Vikings, soldiers, etc.); sports stars (baseball players, football players, etc.); pirates; cowboys; policemen; firemen; pilots; astronauts; spies; and the like.

ACCEPTABLE BUT NOT PREFERRED COSTUMES: doctors, businessmen, construction workers, farmers, and the like.

UNACCEPTABLE COSTUMES: anything inhibiting clear vision (large hats, hard-to-see-through masks, dark goggles, etc.); anything inhibiting the ability to maneuver (gowns, capes, flappy pants, shoes with bulky or weird shoes, bulky or padded clothing, etc.); anything "girly" (Barbie, princesses, etc.); anything "little kid" (Care Bears, Thomas the Tank Engine, Smurfs, *Sesame Street* characters, etc.); and the like.

After reviewing their shared costume expectations, which are really more *guidelines* than *rules* (having broken from them on occasion), they return to trick-or-treating planning. They begin discussing the most important topic, the optimal TOTR. As the others gather around, Phil rolls out onto the yellowed, plywood-topped workbench the map he started last night for this year's route. He has attempted to incorporate "fixes" for the mistakes made last year. Smoothing out the map a few times with his hands, Phil begins to run through the route in detail. He explains how this route solves the timing mistakes and delays they encountered last year. He reminds everyone that they *must* have the will-power to move on from the Hotters' house quicker. Getting to Cherry Grove as soon as possible is the top goal. He highlights the key stops and pathways along the route in their neighborhood prior to them traversing the Clarks' yard. The others, mostly Mike, add minor comments and suggestions here and there, but for the most part Phil has figured everything out to perfection. Mooch starts getting very excited and almost starts drooling as he thinks of all the candy they're going to accumulate this year.

Finalizing the first portion of the route, Phil takes a long sigh and then states nervously, "Well, guys, the toughest part is figuring out how to get through the Clarks' yard alive. Still haven't solved that. I have some ideas, but—"

"We should just all run through there as fast as we can," blurts Cruz.

"I think we can come up with more of a plan than that," replies Phil, smirking.

"Plus, not all of us can run fast, or even kind of fast," adds Mike as he looks over at Mooch.

"Yeah, I'm not liking that idea so much," says Mooch. "I veto it based on my last-Halloween-here-ever veto power. If we only had some recon information to help us plan this," he continues in a garbled voice, his mouth full of M&M's.

Mooch is sarcastically referring to earlier in the week, when Phil and Cruz were assigned with and accordingly attempted to perform reconnaissance at the Clarks' house. Very little, if any, recon was accomplished because a few minutes into the mission, while standing in front of the house, they heard "loud and scary" noises and thus became frightened and ran away.

Defending himself and Cruz, Phil tells the story in more detail, attempting to provide an "acceptable" excuse, but Mooch and Mike are having no part of it. Cruz remains silent. He never has and never will admit to being scared of anything or anyone. The conversation heats up as Phil and Mooch exchange jabs, highlighting each others' deficiencies at everything from planning to eating too much to playing baseball to being scared. After allowing the nonsense to go on for a few minutes, Mike finally cuts it off, reminding them that they don't have time to waste arguing about such things.

Each takes a few moments of silence to gather himself and refocus on the important task at hand. Phil breaks the quiet by sharing a couple ideas he's been thinking about for traversing the Clarks' yard. The others listen intently and quickly agree that Phil's ideas are good in concept. He asks the others to give him a little more time to refine them and promises to have them ready in time for Halloween.

Moving on to the last important topic, Phil states that he believes he's devised a foolproof plan to set a trap for Josh's Crew. They'll stage a false candy-storage location! A plan that will not only trick (and piss off) Josh and his crew, but also distract and stall them while they make their way through the Clarks' yard to Cherry Grove. Everyone *loves* this idea. They huddle excitedly around Phil as he explains all the details.

Meanwhile, the girls have convened at their favorite after-school hangout, Dona's Doughnut Shop, where, even with upbeat pop music echoing in the background, the mood on this day is gloomier than usual. Today Lisa isn't her typical witty conversationalist. She's down about Mike cancelling their plan to trick-or-treat together this year. She hasn't even touched her beloved French cruller. Terry, on the other hand, is halfway through her chocolate-iced chocolate cake doughnut, while Roni nibbles on her sprinkle-topped glazed doughnut.

"Come on, Lisa. Cheer up. It's going to be okay. We're going to have a great time trick-or-treating together. It'll be more fun with just us anyway. We can do what we want to do, how and when we want to do it," says Roni, attempting to console her friend.

With her head buried in her crossed arms that are resting on the bright-pink plastic laminate topped table, Lisa lets out a long, loud sigh and then and bows her head in mild agreement.

"Yeah, we didn't need those boys to control and ruin our trick-or-treating anyway," adds Terry. "They're too particular about their route, and they're always rushing from house to house in a big hurry. We can take our time, and we'll get to see other people more."

"Like Josh, perhaps?" asks Roni teasingly.

"No! I'm just saying it will be better not to be stuck with Mike's Gang all night, having to listen to Mooch's nonsense."

"Uh-huh. You do like the way Mooch is so attentive to you, though. You would enjoy that," continues Roni.

"Ha! No thanks," responds Terry, waving her hand at Roni is dismissal.

"Well, I wouldn't have minded hanging out with them—they're fun and nice. And I like it when Cruz shares his candy with me," Roni admits.

"By *shares* you mean trades, right?" pokes Terry.

"Yeah, I guess," responds Roni, smiling proudly and fondly remembering her trading Cruz a kiss for candy a year or so ago. "It was a good trade. You thinking of copying it with Josh?"

"No! No!" retorts Terry. "Well . . . maybe."

"You would really trade a kiss with Josh for candy?! Wow! News alert: Terry has officially broken through her shell and is admitting that boys are cute!" exclaims Roni, causing Lisa to lift her head slightly and crack a small smile.

"No! Not that! I mean, maybe we should all go together with Josh and his crew. They can be fun too and it would probably make Mike jealous."

"And Mooch?" adds Roni jokingly.

"I don't think I want to get involved in another one of your elaborate covert plots, Terry. Honestly, I'm still hoping Mike will change his mind," says Lisa sadly as she raises her head off the table and leans back onto the bright-red leather of the booth to engage the others.

"Oh, I know. But I don't know if that's going to happen with it being Mooch's last year here and all. You know how tight Mike's Gang is; he can't let his friend down," Roni offers in a tone that's as mild as possible.

"Yeah, probably. But he *always* goes with them. He's had so many years with his friends. After thinking it over for a while, he may decide it's time to move past that phase of his life. I know he wants to go with me," Lisa continues.

"Yeah, I think he does too. I just think he's torn—he's in a tough spot," adds Roni.

"Well, he shouldn't have said yes to me in the first place. And he shouldn't have gone back on his promise to me," replies Lisa, now shifting away from sadness, closer to anger.

"Yeah, he shouldn't renege on you like that—that was kind of mean," prods Terry, trying to stoke Lisa's anger. "You going to eat your doughnut?"

Under the brightly lit, faux-crystal chandelier hanging over the center of the table, Lisa shakes her head as she slides her doughnut over to Terry and then exclaims, "Right?! Not cool! Not nice!"

After glaring for a second or two at Terry, who's now consumed with devouring Lisa's doughnut, Roni attempts to calm Lisa. "Maybe. But I think we should just move on and concentrate on having fun by ourselves."

"Yeah, probably . . . But it still does make me mad . . . He reneged on me, on *me*!" exclaims Lisa.

"Yeah, I guess so," replies Roni, now somewhat unsure about giving Mike the benefit of the doubt as her protective nature kicks in.

"Well I still think going with Josh is a good plan—I mean, it's an idea worth considering," concludes Terry.

As Terry and Roni finish their doughnuts, Lisa's mind spins, contemplating whether Mike will change his mind or not, how much time she should give him, and what and when her next move should be.

9

Trick-or-Treating Memories

In an act never witnessed before, Mooch and Terry arrive to lunch *together*. Stopping just outside the lunchroom door to finish their conversation, Mooch is displaying his typical awkward and sheepish behavior (like every time he's around Terry), while Terry is projecting her typical arrogant and condescending attitude (like every time she's around Mooch). But this time their typical mannerisms are noticeably exaggerated—Mooch amplifying his vulnerability to facilitate some kind of benefit and Terry acting like she's attaining something of great significance. After wrapping up their chat, they pass through the door and unceremoniously separate, casually waving good-bye to each other. Terry heads toward her friends, while Mooch walks over to Mike and Cruz. Phil still hasn't arrived.

Approaching his friends puffed up with an uncharacteristic aura of accomplishment, Mooch sits down at the table next to Mike. "How do you do, gentlemen?"

"Gentlemen?! What's up with you today?" asks Mike as Cruz peers at Mooch like he's lost his mind.

Smiling back at them triumphantly, Mooch replies with a big smile, "You're right. Sorry. You two are no gentlemen."

Not liking this comment, Cruz reaches across the table and smacks Mooch on the side of the head.

"Ow! That was uncalled for. I was just joking," states Mooch as he rubs his head to ease the pain.

"What's with you and Terry showing up together?" asks Mike. "What were you guys talking about in the hallway?"

"Yeah, weird, huh? Oh . . . Nothing, she just had another question about science class. No big deal."

"She's had a lot of questions lately about science class. Seems like kind of a *big deal*," continues Mike.

"She's just not that good at science."

"And *you* are?"

"Ha! Well, not exactly . . . But, better than her I guess."

While Mike is once again uneasy about a conversation between Mooch and Terry and feeling compelled to continue this line of questioning, he succumbs to the realization that Mooch is not going to divulge the true content of their exchange and accordingly lets it go.

"Lunchtime! Finally!" exclaims Phil as he arrives to the table and covertly slants an inquisitive glance at Mooch before sitting next to Cruz.

Mooch subtly nods back—Mike and Cruz not noticing, being more interested in food—and replies in garbled voice, his mouth full of food, "Yessir, the best period of the day."

With all members now present and commencing their meal, the gang's excitement for trick-or-treating immediately explodes as they relive some of their past great adventures.

The Hot Year

Phil recalls the dreadful year when, due to the extreme heat, much of their candy melted in their bags before they could eat it.

"Mooch almost had a coronary! Never seen someone so mad in all my life!"

Shaking his head as he lowers it to look down solemnly at the table, Mooch replies in a regrettable tone, "That was horrible. It was a candy massacre. I still get chills down my spine thinking about it—the horror, the carnage, so much good candy squandered that day."

"Yeah, but it didn't stop you, did it?" continues Phil.

"Well, I just couldn't give up, it was *chocolate*. I had to exhaust all options to save it. I had to attempt anything and everything."

"Yeah, by the end of your attempts, your hands, face, and shirt were completely covered in chocolate. Not sure much actually made it into your mouth!" adds Mike.

"Ha! Yeah, I remember the chocolate melting off of your face and running down your neck! What a mess!" continues Phil.

"Well, most made it into my mouth, but a bunch was all over my body! I think some may have even made it down into my underwear by the time we got home—my mom was not pleased, at all. But, hey, you have to take risks in life if you want to reap rewards, no matter how ugly it may get."

"It got ugly all right," says Mike.

"You looked like a life-size chocolate Easter bunny!" piles on Phil, laughing loudly.

"Like an evil super villain—chocolate man!" continues Mike, now laughing louder than Phil.

As the forecast for this Halloween calls for it to be hot, Mooch is worried about the possibility their candy might melt again and asks, "You sure those cooler compartments in the backpacks are going to work?"

"Of course they are. My mom's almost got them done," replies Phil confidently.

"Good. I can't handle another awful experience like that," proclaims Mooch. "Thinking more about how hot it's probably going to be and how we won't have a stash site. I wonder if maybe we should double-back halfway through the TOTR and unload candy at Cruz's house?"

Knowing this would obviously take too much time and having already agreed upon most of the TOTR, now getting close to finalizing the details, the others refuse to respond to Mooch's annoying suggestion and just continue on to the next memory.

The Mooch Meltdown Year

Cruz begins to laugh recalling Mooch's meltdown after he accidentally stepped on his costume's cape, causing him to trip and fall as he was running up to the Hotters' porch. The impact with the ground not only tore a hole in his pants and scraped his knee, but also ripped a hole in his bag, causing an unnoticed slow leak of candy dripping out of it throughout the night.

"I think it registered a five on the Richter scale when you hit the ground," says Cruz.

"Ha! Yeah! And you were *so* mad you lost all that candy that you decided to steal and eat a bunch of your sister's candy when you got home—ended up getting grounded by your mom for a month!" recalls Phil, laughing.

After taking a bite out of his peanut butter and jelly sandwich, with his mouth full of food Mooch replies in a garbled voice, "Yeah, I got grounded. But it was worth it! She wasn't going to eat it all anyway. She never does. I prevented it from going to waste. I provided an important community service. I wouldn't change a thing if I had to do it all over again."

The others laugh, knowing that it was truly worth it for Mooch—getting grounded was a small price to pay for an opportunity to enjoy mass quantities of candy.

Phil's Mom-Made Costume Year

Having enough of the teasing at his expense, Mooch fires back at Phil, "How about a couple years ago when your mom made your 'awesome' costume? Had to be *the* worst costume ever!"

The others laugh along with Mooch, and even Phil chuckles a little, responding, "Yeah, can't argue with that. I was hoping for Chewbacca and ended up looking like a giant fur ball come to life. I couldn't see anything at all!"

"A Russian-fur-coat ball of fur," adds Mike, recalling that Phil's mom had made the costume out of old Russian hats she'd found at the second-hand store.

"The look of the costume wasn't the worst part—it did look somewhat like Chewy. Well, probably more like a giant Ewok," says Mooch. "The worst part was that it was *too hot*. Halfway through the route you were soaked with sweat—you nearly passed out! You were a sweaty mess, hair all messed up. Classic!"

Now all laughing loudly, even Phil, he replies, "I know! And, I couldn't get it off for a while! Remember, it had that old zipper my mom sewed in the back that got stuck? I thought I was going to melt away to nothing being trapped inside that costume. You guys were trying like crazy to break it free for what seemed like forever! Ugh, that was horrible."

"I can still see, as clear as day in mind, you eventually tearing the costume, the zipper finally breaking apart, and you scampering around, trying to kick it off your legs in a huge hurry! Like you were on fire!" replies Mike.

"I was *dying* from the heat—could not get it off quick enough."

"Yeah! And then you spent the rest of the night trick-or-treating in your white T-shirt, light-blue shorts, dark-brown knee-high socks, and hiking boots with the costume draped over your shoulder!" yells Mooch laughing hysterically.

"Yeah!" says Mike laughing uncontrollably. "It was like we were suddenly trick-or-treating with one of our dads in his 'doing yardwork' outfit. Ha!"

Bad-Trade Year

Now reaching the end of *his* tolerance for being teased, Phil quickly changes the subject. He reminds everyone of the year Cruz traded to Roni Martinez twenty, yes *twenty*, pieces of his chocolate candy for just one—yes, just *one*—kiss on the cheek. A bit of intel that was conveyed to Mooch by his little sister, who learned it from Roni's little sister.

With Cruz clearly irritated by Phil's reminder, they all sit still in uncomfortable silence. Mike and Mooch anxiously look at Phil, then Cruz, then Phil, then Cruz, and so on, wondering how Cruz will react. To their relief, Cruz says and does nothing, simply glaring unhappily at Phil.

Gulping in mild fear, but sensing Cruz will not retaliate, Phil attempts to walk back his statement, "But I'm sure you gave her all your *worst* pieces."

"We've all had our moments. All great times. I'm sure we'll have even more this year," says Mike, diffusing the situation as they all gather their things to head out to the playground for a game of hoops.

10

Lisa Plots Revenge

Lisa is angry. Angry that Mike has backed out on her this year and angry about all the time she's spent assembling her Wonder Woman costume (the perfect match for Mike's Superman costume).

How dare he turn me *down*, she thinks to herself. *How could he choose going with* those *guys* over *going with* me? *What is he thinking?!*

She's equally sad. Sad that Mike has chosen his friends over her and finding herself still hoping he'll change his mind. She was very much looking forward to spending the evening with him, envisioning them walking along holding hands, talking, and laughing.

"Oh, I wish he would come to his senses already. We'd have such a great time."

Moving back and forth between the two emotions, she finds herself swinging endlessly on an agonizing mental pendulum. Having spent the better part of the day consumed by this predicament, by the afternoon she's weary and decides to take action.

Attempting to suppress her anger, she focuses on ways to coerce Mike into changing his mind. She begins running through the typical tactics.

She'll entice him with her beauty by wearing parts of her Wonder Woman costume to school to give him a glimpse of what he'll be missing. After pondering for a while, she abandons the idea, unable to devise a way to pull it off without looking too obvious.

She'll embarrass him by spreading the word at school that he's broken his promise to go trick-or-treating with her. Being known as a person who keeps his word, Mike will have no choice but to protect his reputation and go with her then. *Nah, too risky. It could backfire if he becomes more angry than embarrassed. It may push him away for good.*

She'll instill conflict in his gang so they'll disband, leaving Mike free to go with her—believing that, if not for their peer pressure, Mike would definitely prefer going with her. *Won't work—his gang is too tight, their bond is too strong, and this year they're too focused since it's Mooch's "last year" and all.* Plus, she couldn't live with herself knowing that she was the one who dismantled their friendship. It's just not her style.

She'll get Roni and Terry to create a distraction for his friends early in the night and then "steal" him away. Once she gets him alone with her, he'll forget about his friends and they'll have a magical evening. *No good—there is no way his friends will let that happen, not on Halloween and certainly not this year.*

Unable to think of a way to persuade Mike into changing his mind, she becomes frustrated and her anger resurfaces. *He has to pay for what he's done to me. He can't just get away with this.* She decides the only surefire way to get his attention is to take Terry's advice. Although it's against her better judgment, she decides to revert to the oldest, simplest, and most effective technique known—jealousy. She'll ask his archenemy to go trick-or-treating with her. She'll ask Josh Pealy!

Knowing Josh wouldn't pass up on this opportunity to stick it to Mike, she figures with a little enticement, he'll surely and eagerly say yes. Plus, knowing that Josh is much more into scheming evil plans than he is into girls, she feels relief that there should be no uncomfortable expectations it'll be a real date—no emotional investment, strictly business. *Perfect plan!*

Conveniently, Lisa is just leaving the girls' locker room for PE class—the same one Josh has. After entering the gymnasium, she immediately spots Josh straight ahead talking to his friend and right-hand man, Bobby Poda. With everyone milling about just waiting for the teacher to arrive, this is the perfect time to ask.

"Hey there, Josh," she says in her "happy" voice.

"Hey," responds Josh in his "cool" voice, taken a bit off guard by her approaching him.

"Can I ask you something in private really quick?"

"Sure," he says, motioning to Bobby to walk away.

As Bobby turns to retreat, she continues, "I was wondering if you'd like to go trick-or-treating with me this year."

Repeating the question in her head again, she fears it may have sounded too intimate or personal and quickly switches gears, blurting out, "With me, Roni, and Terry, I mean. Just thought it would be fun to mix it up a little this year."

Having already heard from Terry that Mike backed out on going with Lisa, Josh immediately thinks to himself, *This is perfect!* Everyone knows Lisa is Mike's crush. So, if he goes with her and Mike finds out, Mike *won't* be happy *at all*. The added bonus is that Lisa is *hot*! It'll be fun to walk around with her all night.

Just as he's ready to respond yes, he realizes Lisa and her friends will most likely slow his crew down. With a full schedule this year—so much candy to gather and steal—he wonders if this opportunity of getting to Mike is worth it in the end. Also, will Lisa and her friends approve of his crew's goal to pilfer as much candy as possible from others and the tactics they'll use to accomplish it?

Carefully weighing all the pros and cons, Josh concludes he can't pass on such a tremendous opportunity to get under Mike's skin. "Yeah, that sounds good."

"Great. I'll let the girls know," Lisa replies. "What's your costume?"

"Batman."

"Perfect. See you later, Batman," Lisa says as she turns to walk toward Roni. She decides she'll now go as Catwoman—the icing on the cake of jealousy for Mike.

"What was that about?" asks Roni.

"I can't let Mike off the hook for reneging on me. I decided to take Terry's advice."

"You did?!"

"Yes. What Mike did wasn't nice, and he has to pay for it. Right?"

Still conflicted, Lisa's now rethinking her decision, wondering if her planned revenge will push Mike too far.

After taking a couple of seconds to think it over, Roni sees the anguish in her best friends face and emphatically responds, "Right!"

"Right . . . Now for the next step. Josh is going as Batman, so I need to change my costume to Catwoman."

"Yeah, tonight we'll make the *best* Catwoman costume this town has ever seen."

11

Test Run and Candy Recon

Arriving directly from school, all four members of the gang have gathered again in Mike's backyard clubhouse and are seated in a circle in the middle of the floor. It's still early in the afternoon. The chandelier is off, as the sunshine beaming through the two windows that flank the entry door provide plenty of light. Mooch is compacted into a worn-out, brown, leather beanbag as he devours a large handful of Oreos he commandeered just a moment ago from Mike's cupboard. The others are hunched over the map rolled out on the floor, intently discussing the TOTR. The discussion has become heated between Phil and Mike as they debate a few unresolved items.

For some locations on the route, the two have differing opinions about what candy will be handed out and when. Accordingly, they also have differing opinions on when these houses should or should not be visited. Mike typically entrusts the planning decisions to Phil, but the pressure of making this year's trick-or-treating the best ever compels him to speak up after suspecting a potential mistake.

Phil, as is typical, gets defensive when his plan is questioned—and for good reason. The vast majority of his past TOTR designs have led to much success. He takes great pride in and puts many hours of thought, often late into the night, into his planning. Phil will consider changing plans when a sound argument is given, but so far, he hasn't been convinced. He maintains that his planning is solid.

After a few more minutes of heated debate, Mike makes progressively insightful points. Phil begins to soften slowly, acknowledging the timing of the route may be off slightly in a couple of spots. He's also feeling pressure to ensure every *t* is crossed and every *i* is dotted this year. As a compromise, Mike suggests they do a TOTR test run on their bikes to check it out. The others agree. Well, all except Mooch, who's still completely consumed with finishing off the Oreos and virtually unaware an argument is taking place.

Continuing the theme of gathering as much information as possible, Phil suggests they also stake out the grocery store to gather intel on what types of candy the moms are buying this year. He argues that the test run combined with this candy recon will provide the information they need to make an informed final decision on the TOTR. His attention caught by the word *candy* in Phil's last sentence, Mooch immediately shifts his attention to their conversation as he places the last cookie into his mouth.

"Today is the best day to spy on the moms at the grocery store," blurts Mooch in a muddled voice, his mouth still half full.

"Why is that?" asks Phil.

"Because today's Super Coupon Day. Today they'll have the mega savings on all candy. *All* the moms know. All of them—well, for sure most of them—will be there, guaranteed!"

The others, dumbfounded that Mooch would know such a thing, can do nothing more than stare at him for a few seconds. Mooch has *always* hated shopping; he *never* goes to the store.

"All the moms and *you*?" replies Phil, confused.

"How do *you* know this?" asks Mike.

"Guys. I make it a point to know everything about candy, especially Halloween candy. Knowing where, when, and how to buy it is crucial to staying on top. It's my job, my duty. You know this," says Mooch, dumbfounded the others need this reminder.

The others concede it makes sense that Mooch would know such things and then they all decide both tasks, the test run and candy recon, must be performed. And based on Mooch's valuable information, they must be performed today. As such, they commence a lengthy discussion on who should go where.

"I'll do the grocery store recon. I don't have the energy for the TOTR test run," says Mooch, lying on his back with his right hand caressing his now-full stomach.

"There may not be any candy left for the moms to buy if you get there first," replies Phil, snickering. "And I'm afraid you might try to mug a mom or two outside the store and steal their candy!"

"Yeah, and then there'd be no candy for the trick-or-treaters," says Mike laughingly.

"Very funny. All of a sudden everyone's a comedian?!" retorts Mooch.

"Well, I'm just saying I'm not sure you can stay focused on the moms and not be distracted by the candy," continues Mike, still laughing.

Cruz just shakes his head, signaling that he doesn't believe Mooch can control himself.

After a few more moments of laughter by all but Mooch, Mike looks at him and concludes, "Well, it'll be getting dark in a couple hours and the test-run team is going to have to move fast. So that pretty much takes you out of consideration for that task—especially in your current condition," referring to his nearly comatose, Oreo-filled state, still lying flat out on the floor.

"Exactly!" exclaims Mooch, shouting up toward the ceiling.

"Okay, Mooch is on the grocery-store recon team," states Phil. "Who's his partner?"

"Well, Cruz and I are the fastest on bikes, so we should probably take the test run," argues Mike as Cruz nods in agreement.

"Yeah, but you two are better at controlling the Cookie Monster," replies Phil, pointing at Mooch. "My riding is fast enough; we have enough time."

"Cookie Monster, ha!" says Cruz.

Mike takes a moment, thinking to himself that Phil probably won't be able to control Mooch at a grocery store full of candy and thus, that task will most likely go unaccomplished. He convinces himself that

Phil will be able to keep up sufficiently on a bike, considering he has a strong vested interest in solving the TOTR argument. Plus, Phil is the master planner and he has virtually every inch of the route memorized.

"Okay, Cookie Monster and Cruz will go to the grocery store. Phil and me on the test run. Let's roll," proclaims Mike as the others quickly jump to their feet, and Mooch slowly rolls to his.

Phil and Cruz immediately race out the door and run home to get their bikes as Mooch follows sluggishly. They return within minutes to Mike's driveway—Mooch with a couple more Oreos taken from his own house in his right hand and one being crunched on inside his mouth.

"Really?" says Phil. "*More* cookies?"

"May as well play the part. And I'm going to need the energy," replies Mooch, smiling as the others laugh and Cruz playfully shoves him in the arm.

"Okay, let's do this, guys. Meet back here just before dark, and *no* messing around," says Mike as they race off—Mike and Phil to the east, Mooch and Cruz to the west.

As Mike and Phil speed through the route, it quickly becomes apparent to both that they must move the timing of their stop at the new rumored-to-be-"rich" and therefore anticipated-to-be-great house. If not, too much time will be squandered in the doubling-back that would be required. Continuing along, they identify a few other minor problem points and discuss possible solutions.

With the sun now barely peeking over the low rolling hills on the horizon, Mike and Phil sit on their bikes and stare at the Clarks' house. The normally white siding is nearly black from the impending darkness, engulfed in a metaphorical blanket of horror. They try to study the details of the yard for anything that may help them traverse it safely, but can't make out too much due to the low light. The longer they stay, the more they begin to see images in the darkness and hear distant screams or shrieks coming from the house or backyard or elsewhere. Unsure if what they're seeing and hearing is real or just their imaginations, they grow more frightened with each passing second. Not wanting to press their luck, they ride off quickly. On the way home they agree that they must get back to Mike's clubhouse to finalize their plan, *tonight*.

Meanwhile, upon arriving at the grocery store, Mooch immediately focuses on buying the candy located at the front of the store near the cash registers. Cruz has to talk him into maintaining his focus, physically holding Mooch's head with both hands and turning him toward the back of the store, where they can better keep a low profile and stealthily observe. Reluctantly, Mooch agrees and the two migrate quickly to the far corner.

The first mom to arrive is Mrs. Anchor, who purchases her typical high-quality selection of awesome candy. All good so far! Shortly thereafter, Mrs. Hotter, Mrs. Gully, and others show up one by one with coupons in hand to purchase their Halloween candy. Mooch was right—son of a gun!

With most of the moms having passed through with no real surprise purchases observed and the sun setting quickly, the boys decide it's time to go. As they walk toward the front of the store, they overhear a conversation between Mrs. Winny and another mom in the next row over, causing them to abruptly stop in their tracks to listen intently. The conversation provides a crucial piece of information, a golden nugget of intel that could affect the route. It must be discussed with the others ASAP. They wait for the conversation between the moms to end and then quickly and quietly scamper out of the grocery store—Mooch taking an agonized, mouth-watering parting gaze at the candy underneath the cashier counter.

As they mount their bikes, they see the new and rumored-to-be- "rich" parents enter the store. They briefly contemplate going back in to see what types of candy they're buying, but they can't contain their excitement about telling their friends what they've already learned. They decide to forego any further reconnaissance and leave.

Mike and Phil arrive back at the clubhouse first and immediately unroll the TOTR map to make the necessary modifications that reflect the valuable information gathered during their test run. No longer at odds, they're in complete agreement on what must be done and are laser focused on finalizing the map. Growing more and more excited for Halloween, and now very confident in their plan, they feel a strong and very satisfying sense of accomplishment. Doing the test run was exactly what they needed!

About fifteen minutes later, Mooch and Cruz arrive. Cruz is partially, and Mooch completely, out of breath from the fast bike ride back. Mooch attempts to share what they saw and overheard at the grocery store, but he can't catch his breath enough to do so. Cruz takes over and quickly summarizes the critical pieces of information as Mooch collapses to floor, lying flat out on his back and gasping for air. Listening intently to what Cruz has to say, Mike and Phil become equally excited and give the grocery-store recon team BIG high fives. The gang then huddles around the TOTR map as Mike and Phil explain what they learned on their journey and the modifications they've already made. They invite Cruz and Mooch to help incorporate the finishing touches.

"That should do it, boys!" proclaims Phil with great pride as he ceremoniously makes the final mark on the map.

"A job well done by all!" says Mike. "I'm proud of you, Cookie Monster," he says, referring to Mooch's ability to control himself at the grocery store.

"Yeah, Cruz only had to corral me once. Surprised even me," replies Mooch as Cruz messes up his hair.

"I'm guessing that eating an entire bag of Oreos before heading out probably helped control your urges," adds Phil.

"Maybe a tiny bit," replies Mooch. "But it was still tough for me to walk by all that delicious candy just begging me to snatch it up."

"There was a trail of drool behind him as we left," jokes Cruz.

Mooch nods. "True."

After standing up and sharing another round of high fives, Phil rolls up the map, secures it with a rubber band, and carefully places it in a special hidden sleeve inside his backpack. They file out of the club-house, through the gate to the front yard, and onto Mike's driveway. Reaching the sidewalk, Mooch recalls one more piece of information.

"Oh, yeah! I almost forgot! We saw the new rich parents walk into the grocery store as we were leaving—looked like they were there to buy some candy too. So that's a good sign!"

"Did you see what kind of candy they were buying?" asks Phil, irritated this information wasn't disclosed prior to finalizing the TOTR map.

"No, it was getting dark and we wanted to get back as soon as we could to tell you guys what we heard from Mrs. Winny," replies Mooch.

"Argh! It would've been nice to know. It would've just taken you a few more minutes to find out. It could affect the route," says Phil, now more aggravated.

Mooch and Cruz look at each other and then look back at Mike and Phil, shrugging their shoulders with no good response to offer.

"Well, we got a lot of good information today anyway. We'll just stick to the plan, assuming they'll have good candy like we think," concludes Mike.

As the trio rides off to their houses, Mike turns around to head to-ward his house and laughs to himself, able to hear Phil and Mooch still arguing in the distance. Being a perfectionist, Phil can't let go of the notion that not having the new neighbor information makes the plan incomplete. Mooch on the other hand, feels Phil is being overdramatic and annoying with his unrealistic expectation for perfection.

"Just relax, Phil. It'll all work out just fine. How much differ-ence could this little detail make?" Mooch reassures him. "All that recon made me *hungry*."

12

Near Map Theft

As they start their journey home after school, Mooch immediately begins devouring strands of Twizzlers chocolate licorice, rapidly taking small quick bites in a machine-gun style as he methodically presses the end of each strand against his front teeth. With his mouth full of tiny pieces of licorice, he takes a break in between strands to lament *again* about Josh's Crew stealing their loot last year. He relives it in agonizing detail, emphatically expressing his extreme disapproval of and anger toward the act, and then concludes *again* with the proclamation that they *must* achieve revenge. The others, having heard this now for the three-hundred-and-seventy-ninth time (give or take), remain silent and simply shake their heads affirmatively in silence.

Mooch shifts his focus to complaining about some of the other things he dislikes about Josh and his goons: "They have no goodness in them. They're pure evil, bullying every kid in the neighborhood all the time. But worse, they have absolutely no respect for Halloween. None at all! I wish I could make them memorize and live by the Trick-or-Treating Code. Or better yet, maybe hypnotize them into following it."

"Maybe write it on paper and feed it to them," suggests Cruz.

Mooch then proceeds to recite their Trick-or-Treating Code as the others quickly join in. "Respect the houses—be courteous, be thankful!

"Respect the candies—all sacred, none wasted!

"Respect the costumes—keep 'em pristine, keep 'em clean!" Mike, Phil, and Cruz point at Mooch as they say the last phrase, recognizing his consistent inability, not for lack of trying, to adhere to this.

"Respect the route. Keep to the course, keep to the plan!"

Then as is their custom, Mooch concludes with, "And above all, respect the *chocolate*, for it is the Candy of the Gods!" Followed by a collective laugh and high fives all around.

Cruz is the first to exit the group since his house is closest to school. He says good-bye in his usual fashion—no words, just a simple wave. Mooch and Mike are next-door neighbors and second to peel off. They say their good-byes to Phil, jokingly making sure all his clothes are property aligned and patting down his hair before letting him on his way. Walking away, Phil intentionally untucks his shirt and messes up his hair, prompting Mooch to yell, "Come on, Phillip! We had you looking so nice!" followed by a parting laugh.

Phil passes the house just past Mike's and turns the corner toward his house, which is a few lots down on the left. With his head down, deep in thought about anything he may have missed on the TOTR as well as how to avenge what Josh's Crew did to them last year, he walks slowly down the dimly lit sidewalk. With Halloween only one day away, he's really feeling the pressure. He holds himself solely responsible for developing flawless plans, plans that facilitate gathering large quantities of great candy, plans that will avenge the gang, plans that will send Mooch off properly.

"Hey!"

Startled, Phil abruptly looks up and takes a small jump backward as his heart skips a beat in fear. It's Josh Pealy standing directly in front of him with one of his goons, Travis Bennett, at his side.

"Give us the map," demands Josh, glaring at Phil as he approaches.

Still trying to restart his heart and regain his breath, Phil takes a moment to gather himself and calmly replies, "What map?"

"GIVE US THE MAP!" demands Josh.

"I'm sorry, I don't know what you're talking about. Map?"

"Look, punk, give us the map. NOW!"

"What are—"

Deciding he's had enough of this chitchat, the much stronger Josh cuts off Phil's sentence, grabbing his backpack by the shoulder strap and spinning him around. With Phil's backpack now easily accessible, Josh unzips the front lower pocket and begins his search. Phil attempts to squirm out of Josh's grasp, but Travis quickly jumps in to hold his arms by his side to assist in keeping him from working free.

Knowing the map is, in fact, inside his backpack, albeit in a secret compartment, Phil is becoming increasingly worried that Josh will eventually find it. He's desperate for a way to deter Josh, distract him, and wiggle out of this jam. *Josh CANNOT find the map, he CANNOT!* It would ruin all they've worked for—his friends would never forgive him. As his mind frantically spins, attempting to conjure an escape from this situation, he wonders how Josh knows about the map. Their maps have always been super top secret. No one outside the gang has ever uttered a word about their existence, ever.

"I know it's in here!" exclaims Josh, as he now hurriedly unzips and digs through the front upper pocket.

Frustrated by not finding what he's looking for, Josh pushes Travis to the side and works the backpack off of Phil's back, twisting it aggressively back and forth down his arms.

Feeling completely helpless—and realizing Josh will soon find the map—Phil squints his eyes in a last-ditch attempt to force his brain to devise some way, any way, to escape this disastrous situation.

With the backpack now resting on the ground, Josh goes into extreme search mode.

"Find it?" asks Travis.

Josh looks up at him and gives him an irritated look as if to say: *Not yet, but I will if you stop interrupting me.* He turns his eyes back to the backpack to continue his search, but halfway through the motion sees it briskly swooped up off the ground.

"Not so fast!" yells a voice.

Yes! It's Mike! Phil realizes.

"Hey!" replies Josh angrily. "Give it back!"

"I don't think so. It's not yours."

"Give it back *or else.*"

Mike keeps a firm hold on the backpack, staring directly into Josh's eyes as Phil walks over to stand next to him. Although Josh is slightly bigger and stronger than Mike, he's not going to back down to Josh—not tonight, no way. Mike knows Josh isn't going to back down either; once Josh has begun an evil plan, he must finish it. That's a part of his "code." He has a reputation to uphold. The rest of the kids can't view him as nice or weak in any way, at any time.

"You're going to have to take it from me," says Mike, standing his ground, ready for a fight if necessary.

"If you insist," says Josh as he lunges aggressively toward Mike.

Mike quickly jumps to the side, like a matador, causing Josh to pass by and tumble to one knee. After regaining his balance, Josh angrily turns around to face Mike and screams, "Argh!"

"What's going on here?!" yells another approaching voice.

"These goons tore off my backpack and were searching through it!" Phil explains to the approaching Mooch.

"Goons?" replies Travis.

With Phil and Mooch now flanking him on each side, Mike proclaims, "Looks like it's three against two now."

"Three against one and a half," says Mooch, making fun of Travis's small size.

"Hey!" yells Travis.

"One and a quarter?" continues Mooch.

"More like two against four," fires back Travis, now making fun of Mooch's large size.

"Ha!" retorts Mooch sarcastically. "Nice delayed comeback! So delayed I almost forgot what we were talking about."

Josh glares at Mike and then looks back at Travis, taking a moment to reevaluate the situation. Considering his partner is undersized and unreliable, at least when it comes to fighting, he realizes they're outmanned. He decides it's best to not proceed. "Let's go, Trav. We don't need the stupid map anyway. We know how to trick-or-treat as good as they do already."

"C'mon, Josh! We can take *them*!" exclaims Travis, eager to make Mooch eat his words.

Josh turns back to stare into Mike's eyes for a moment, looking for any sign of weakness. Seeing no such sign, he slowly turns back to Travis, pauses, and then begins walking away.

Disappointed, Travis looks at the trio and then turns slowly to follow behind with his head hung low. He let Josh down. If he were as big and tough as Bobby or Rob, things would've probably ended differently.

The gang shares this sentiment—feeling lucky Josh's partner was Travis tonight and not one of the other goons. They all take a collective deep breath and look at each other in relief—crisis averted!

Phil turns to Mike and asks, "How do you think they know about the map? We've always been very good at keeping it a secret in the past."

"That's a really good question," replies Mike while glancing over at Mooch.

Mike doesn't know for sure, but he's fairly certain Mooch is indirectly responsible for them knowing about the map. He's guessing Mooch, vulnerable to Terry's tactics, was manipulated into accidentally leaking the existence of the map to her.

Sensing that Mike knows the mistake he's made and feeling ashamed, Mooch quickly attempts a distraction. "They must be spying on us."

Phil also suspects it was Mooch who divulged the highly sensitive information, recalling previous times he's messed up thanks to Terry's interference. This wouldn't the first time Mooch has given secret information to her and most likely not the last.

With no response from his friends, Mooch figures Phil must also know—no words are required to verify this suspicion. They've been friends long enough that he can just tell.

They walk together in silence to Phil's house to ensure he makes it there safely—Mooch ashamed and the other two disappointed. Reaching Phil's front door, Mooch internally attempts to justify what he did—desperately searching for a validation for his grave mistake. Finding none, he considers admitting to the others what he did, but can't bring himself to confess to his very best friends the terrible error he's committed.

As he separates from Mike to walk up his driveway, he feels he really let his friends down. He vows to redeem himself and regain their trust.

13

Pre~Trick~or~Treat Meeting

With a family-size bag of sour-cream-and-onion potato chips nestled between his crossed legs, Mooch is sitting on the old shag carpeting that covers most of Mike's basement. The bag is wide open to facilitate the giant scoops of chips being transferred rhythmically to his mouth. A routine that has been his pre-trick-or-treating ritual for years now—eating salty snacks before heading out to collect the "mass quantities of sugar." He argues that he must perform this ritual to "neutralize" his body so he can "maximize" his sugar intake throughout the night. The others have witnessed this routine many times before but are still amazed and perplexed by it. They choose instead to fast as much as possible all day long to maximize their sugar intake throughout the night. They spend little time marveling at Mooch's custom, however. More important matters require their attention, such as double- and triple-checking their gear and going over the TOTR map one last time.

Sitting on the old yellow-and-brown-striped couch situated against the light-colored wood-paneled wall, Phil begins to disperse the compartmentalized bags to the others. Upon doing so, he notices that one is torn on the side—introducing an undesired potential candy leak. Knowing that Mike's mom is an expert seamstress, he quickly darts upstairs to seek her out. As he enters the kitchen, he finds her already occupied. She's helping Mike's younger brother Pip with his costume, and by the looks of it, she won't be available any time soon. Notorious for waiting until the very last moment to put together his costume, Pip consumes all of Mike's mom's pre-trick-or-treating time every year—so annoying!

Giving up on this idea, Phil hastily heads back to the basement and commences fixing the tear himself using his very best *MacGyver* (Phil's favorite television show) skills. Taking out his pocketknife, he quickly makes a few small slots on each side of the tear and then grabs an old shoelace from one of the metal storage shelves in the rear of the basement underneath the stairs. Carefully tying the tear together like sewing closed a wound, he completes the sutures with a couple of aggressive tugs and a snug double knot.

"Ready for action! Look at that. Good as new!" he exclaims.

"Nice!" excitedly replies Mike, standing next to the couch now fully outfitted in his Superman costume, cape and all.

"That cape is going to be trouble. It will be a problem if we run into a sticky situation. I'm telling you, it's a bad move," advises Phil.

"I'll take my chances. Can't go as Superman and *not* have a cape—that would make *no* sense. I can wrap it around my neck if I need to."

Mooch is dressed up as the legendary baseball player Babe Ruth, with his rotund belly filling out the costume to perfection. Phil is going as Indiana Jones, donning the iconic dark-brown fedora hat and leather jacket with a brown spray-painted jump rope acting as his whip. Cruz, who has yet to show up, will be The Terminator and allegedly will be wearing dark-black sunglasses, against repeated objections by the others who cite it as a costume violation.

"He'd better not be wearing the sunglasses—he won't be able to see. He'll be putting us all at risk. *Two* violations this year. Bad luck!" exclaims Phil, eyeing Mike's cape again.

"You think I should bring the bat? It may come in handy if we have to fight off Pealy and his band of thugs," asks Mooch holding an old wooden baseball bat.

"No!" reply Mike and Phil simultaneously.

"It will be too much to carry. You'll just end up whining about it all night," continues Mike.

"Wonder what Cruz would think?" murmurs Mooch.

The reason for Cruz's absence is that he's still at school serving detention. A circumstance that will soon elevate the other gang members' anxiety if Cruz remains absent.

Flashback to This Morning

While walking to school, Mike, Phil, and Mooch explain to Cruz how Josh and Travis attempted to steal the TOTR map the night before. As the story progresses, Cruz becomes more and more angry. He's very protective of his friends, and he knows Josh wouldn't have attempted such a thing had he been there. Upon arriving at school, Cruz lets the others go to their homerooms, telling them he'll catch up with them later. He then patiently waits alone for Josh to arrive.

Shortly thereafter, Josh and Bobby arrive together. Upon passing through the front doors, they find Cruz standing there, glaring at them, his arms crossed against his chest.

"Heard you were harassing my friends yesterday? Tried to steal something from them?"

Already somewhat intimidated by Cruz and now recognizing his anger, Josh replies in a calm tone. "Uh . . . Well . . . It wasn't so much 'steal' as it was 'borrow.' We were just kidding around though. We just wanted—"

"I know what you did and I know you weren't kidding and I'm not happy about it. At all!" yells Cruz, cutting off Josh's sentence.

He has never liked these two, or their buddies. They're all bullies, and Cruz absolutely despises that. He tries to stop bullies every chance he gets. With his anger escalating, he shoves Josh back, causing him to fall to the ground and then turns to look at Bobby to see what his move, if any, will be.

Not wanting any part of this situation, particularly at school where a teacher could walk around the corner at any moment, Bobby looks at Cruz for no more than a second before turning and running away down the hallway. Cruz turns his attention back to Josh, who's still on the ground. He moves forward to stand over and glare down at him. As he starts to lean over and point his finger in Josh's face, he hears a voice from down the hallway.

"Hey! What's going on there?!" yells Mr. Frank, the assistant principal and a strict disciplinarian.

As Mr. Frank approaches them, Josh remains on the ground and begins wincing as if he's in tremendous pain.

"He punched me for no reason. Knocked me to the ground," states Josh, giving an Oscar-worthy performance in playing up his "injuries," holding his stomach and groaning in pain.

"That's not true!" replies Cruz.

"So, what is true?" asks Mr. Frank.

"Well, he . . . I just . . . I just shoved him a little," explains Cruz. "He was—"

"A *little*, huh? Looks like it was enough to knock him to the ground."

"Yeah, but—"

"I've heard enough. Mr. Pealy, you're free to leave. Mr. Rivera, please come with me to the principal's office."

Josh picks himself up and gives Cruz a sly look as if to say *Ha, ha!* He then turns in the direction of his homeroom and retreats slowly down the hallway, still playing up his fake injuries by moaning, limping, and holding his stomach in "pain."

Mr. Frank escorts Cruz to the principal's office, lectures him for a while on how he can't "bully" other students in the hallways, and then requires him to serve detention after school.

Detention on HALLOWEEN?! Leaving the principal's office, Cruz is beyond angry, frustrated, and flabbergasted that Josh has once again snowed an adult into believing his lame act and once again gotten the best of him. Dejectedly, he wanders to his homeroom, knowing there's nothing he can do about it. At least for now.

Back to This Afternoon

Mooch, with his salty-snack "neutralization" now complete, suddenly stands up in panic. He's just remembered what Bobby Poda yelled to him on the way over to Mike's house.

"Guys! Oh crap, I forgot. On the way over here, Bobby was across the street and yelled over to me that Cruz's mom told him that Cruz is grounded for getting detention at school today and won't be trick-or-treating with us tonight! You think it's true, Mikey?!" asks Mooch, his voice elevated now in fear.

"That would be awful! Would ruin everything! All we've worked for!" exclaims Phil, believing the story since Bobby's house is close to Cruz's, making it possible that Cruz's mom did convey this information to him.

"Guys. We don't know if it's true, and we don't have time to sit around and worry about it. For now, we have to believe it's *not* true and just stick to the plan," replies Mike calmly, attempting to settle the other two down.

Meanwhile back at school, Cruz sits in a chair in the lunchroom, staring at the clock on the far wall. This clock has never moved slower than it is right now. The same clock that has the audacity to move at lightning speed every day during lunchtime when he and his buddies are enthralled in deep conversations about important topics, such as sports, movies, girls (occasionally), and lately Halloween—particularly, candy. Desperately wanting to leave, thinking of all he has to do prior to trick-or-treating, he's hoping Mr. Frank will let them go early. To encourage this possibility, he sits completely still and silent.

Mr. Frank, however, has never been known to let students go early. He sees "upholding the school rules" as his "civic responsibility and duty." Although he won't admit it, particularly at this moment, this is something that Cruz can't help but respect, having the same opinion of rules and how they should be consistently obeyed by all.

At four thirty sharp (as the second hand ticks exactly on the twelve), Mr. Frank calmly proclaims, "Students, I truly hope you have learned your lesson. Perhaps next time, prior to making a decision to misbehave, you will recollect on the time spent here today and think better of it. Accordingly, I hope not to see you here again. You are free to leave."

Cruz instantly jumps from his chair and runs as fast as he can out the door, down the hallway, out of the school, and toward his home.

Back at Mike's house, the gang knows Cruz won't get out of detention until four thirty or later. Then it will take him about fifteen minutes to get home and about another twenty minutes to get ready and make it over to Mike's. This means he won't convene with the others until a little after five, assuming he isn't grounded. Wanting to leave at exactly five o'clock, this timing complicates things, as Cruz is in charge of bringing an important item, the ice packets that will keep their candy cool. The ice packets that are inconveniently currently stored in the kitchen freezer at his house.

At 4:45 p.m. Mike calls Cruz's house, hoping he's made it there. His mom answers the phone and informs Mike that Cruz still isn't home from school. Mike asks her if she can tell Cruz to meet them in front of the Krisyzniaks' house. Cruz's mom complies, but is short—unusual for Mrs. Rivera, who typically talks *a lot*. Uneasy from her response, or lack thereof, Mike slowly hangs up the phone, wondering whether or not Cruz will be joining them tonight.

Watching every word spoken and every move made by Mike, Mooch and Phil wait impatiently with eyes wide open. Will Cruz be able to meet them, or is he grounded?

"Well?!" asks Phil.

"Hard to say. She said she'll tell him to meet us, but she wasn't her usual talkative—"

"Oh no! He's grounded, I know it! This is going to be the worst farewell tour ever!" exclaims Mooch, holding his head in down his hands.

"Look, let's not jump to conclusions. Let's wait and see. No sense in worrying about it yet," says Mike, again trying to calm the others down.

"Why didn't you ask her if he's grounded?" asks Phil. "We *need* to know! We *need* to plan! You need to call her back and ask. Right now."

"Yeah, call her back and find out!" agrees Mooch.

"Because, I didn't want to tip her off, guys. Didn't want to give her any ideas. Look, Cruz will be there. He's never let us down, ever—and he won't let us down tonight."

As they gather their gear, footsteps can be heard coming down the stairs. It's Pip, dressed up as a pirate.

"Arr! Can I go with you guys tonight, Mike?" he asks in his best, but not very good, pirate voice.

"Just you or your merry band of knuckleheads too?" replies Mike.

"All of us. I can't abandon my buddies."

"Sorry, no can do. You guys would slow us down too much. Plus, it's our last year together, and we want to enjoy it without distractions. It's Mooch's farewell grand-master tour!"

Dejected, Pip turns around and plods his way back up the stairs. The gang follows close behind. Ready to roll, they stop in the kitchen to say their good-byes to Mrs. Hendricks and then head out the front door. They pause on the driveway to collectively recite the Trick-or-Treating Code and then "gear up" (meaning, put their backpacks on) and commence the TOTR, without Cruz, at five o'clock sharp.

14

The Krisyzniaks' and Anchors'

It's on! Trick-or-treating has officially begun and the gang, well three-quarters of it, is pumped up! They make their way quickly through the first group of "minor" houses (those offering average candy) on their way to the first of the "major" houses (those offering exceptional candy). These categories have been established by the gang based on several factors, listed here in order of importance: past experience, intel (information obtained via conversations with others or overhearing conversations by others), recon (information obtained by observation), and gut feel.

The first house of note isn't an official major house, but more of what they call a pre-major house and is positioned in the lineup specifically to obtain a crucial element required at the first true major house. It is the Krisyzniaks' house, which is notorious for handing out cheap plastic Halloween toys. Exactly what they need.

As they approach the driveway, they're immersed in an argument about whether or not this house should be visited. Mike is against it, Phil and Mooch are for it. Opposing points are shot back and forth until they ultimately reach the front porch, at which point Mike relents, figuring a few more steps won't hurt and that he'd rather just get it over with and not waste any more time. Excited, Mooch is the first to arrive at the door. He quickly rings the doorbell. A few seconds later Mrs. Krisyzniak comes to the door with, as anticipated, a large bowl of cheap plastic toys!

"Yes!" says Mooch, pumping his fist. "The official start of HOW-Loween! AHOO!"

"Trick-or-treat!" yells the trio.

"Welcome, trick-or-treaters! You're our first group of the night."

As she reaches into the bowl to grab a handful of items, Mooch and Phil survey the bowl for the articles they desire.

"I see 'em," whispers Mooch to Phil, covering his mouth so as not to let Mrs. Krisyzniak see.

A wide-eyed Phil shakes his head excitedly up and down in agreement. She proceeds to pass out the toys one by one. Phil receives a vampire bat on a string, Mooch a black spider ring, and Mike a glow-in-the-dark skeleton. Not bad toys by typical standards, but they aren't what Phil and Mooch require. Quickly, they initiate their backup plan of distraction and pilfering. Using his very best improvisational skills, Mooch glowingly compliments Mrs. Krisyzniak on her collection of witch dolls sitting on the credenza just inside the room behind her. Flattered by Mooch noticing her beloved dolls, she graciously thanks him and turns around to proudly look upon them as she explains how they were passed down to her from her mother, who received them from her grandmother. In this moment, Phil efficiently and stealthily scans, locates, and snags two sets of vampire teeth from the bowl. Not approving of this mission or these tactics, Mike coughs loudly in an attempt to intentionally sabotage the act, prompting Mrs. Krisyzniak to turn back around quickly. As her vision reconnects with the boys, out of the corner of one eye, she sees Phil's hand completing its move away from the bowl—busted?! Not completely sure of what she has just seen or what is happening, she glares at Phil with a look of suspicion.

"What were you—"

"Trick-or-treat!" screams the next frenzied group of kids bombarding the porch. This creates an opportunistic distraction that offers the perfect opportunity for their escape. Wasting no time in taking full advantage, Phil and Mooch hastily turn and run from the porch, leaving Mike behind.

"That was close!" shouts Mooch as he and Phil reach the end of the driveway.

"Big time!" agrees Phil.

A second or two later, Mike runs up to them and shakes his head in disapproval and disbelief, "You guys! You left me hanging there all alone."

"Had no time to think, just react. Had to take advantage of the window of opportunity. You snooze, you lose," replies Mooch.

Expecting Cruz will meet them here, they impatiently wait for a couple of minutes in the driveway, becoming more and more worried with every tick of Phil's watch.

"Guys, we can't wait anymore. We've got to go. We're going to fall behind the TOTR schedule," pleads Phil.

"Yeah, probably," agrees Mooch, nervously pacing up and down the driveway.

Mike looks at his friends, shaking his head slowly up and down deep in thought, and then turns to look down the street in the direction Cruz should be arriving from. Seeing that he isn't coming, he turns back to face them, pauses, and then says, "Okay, guys. Let's go. Hopefully he meets us at the next stop."

They work their way expeditiously through a couple more minor houses, accumulating various types of mediocre candy, and eventually reach the official start of this year's trick-or-treating—the first major house!

"The Anchors' house!" exclaims Mooch, briskly rubbing his hands together. "Here we go!"

Hoping Cruz will meet them here, they wait on the sidewalk and intently survey the area, but he's nowhere to be found. Having not seen nor heard from him since much earlier in the day back at school, questions start swirling through their heads. *Is he grounded? Is he just late? Is it something else?* After waiting a few moments more with expectant looks up and down the block, they sadly conclude that they must press on without him.

Mooch rings the doorbell. The anticipated *ding-dong* doesn't sound inside the house. Not wanting to ring the doorbell again immediately out of respect, and fearing it may have rung and they just didn't hear it, they wait a few moments. No rustling is heard, and no movement is seen inside. No one is coming? Mike rings the doorbell this time in a more deliberate fashion. Again, no *ding-dong* sound inside the house. Phil peers through the front window, looking for any activity. Lights are on, but no movements, no sounds, no nothing. *How can this be?!*

A look of fear washes over Mooch's face as he concludes the doorbell must be broken! The only other explanation is that the Anchors aren't home! A tragic scenario to contemplate. "This is bad. This is a bad omen, a bad sign. This is *not* the way to kick off trick-or-treating!" Mooch is PISSED, assuming they're going to miss out on this house's amazing treasure.

"Looks that way. And Cruz still isn't here . . . ," replies Phil, who's becoming dejected.

"Cruz will be here, Phil! Mooch, take a deep breath, suck it up, and settle down!" exclaims Mike, attempting to calm his buddies once again.

Just as Mike finishes his sentence, Cruz suddenly appears.

"Sorry, guys . . . it took me a while . . . to convince my mom . . . to let me go," says Cruz, out of breath from running as fast as he could to catch up to them.

After aiming an I-told-you-so look at Mooch and Phil, Mike turns to Cruz. "Great to have you with us, buddy!"

"Yeah, great news. But what are we going to do about the dumb broken doorbell?" complains Mooch.

As Cruz passes out the ice packets and the others carefully place them in their backpacks, Mooch continues his doom-and-gloom monologue about how the night has started off badly and, by all indications, will continue in this manner. Mike and Cruz attempt to calm Mooch's hysterics, but Phil pays no attention. Rather than watch this familiar scene play out *again*, he shifts into full problem-solving mode. Closely examining the doorbell, Phil discovers the button is stuck, jammed by a small twig that is preventing it from performing its usual function.

As Mike, Mooch, and Cruz continue their conversation, Phil methodically pulls a pair of needle-nose pliers from his backpack, carefully removes the twig, puts the pliers away, and calmly rings the doorbell. *DING-DONG.*

Mike, Mooch, and Cruz stop their discussion instantly, turn their heads, and stare in wonder at Phil triumphantly standing with his arms crossed in front of his chest.

Waiting silently in anticipation, after a second or two they hear stirring inside the house and then see silhouettes in the front window.

Yes! they think to themselves, awaiting something fantastic! The door opens to reveal Mr. Anchor dressed in his typical smoking jacket and carrying his signature pipe.

"Trick-or-treat!" shouts the foursome.

"Happy Halloween, gentlemen!" Mr. Anchor replies with a big smile on his face. "Nice costumes!"

He reaches for a wide and shallow bowl full of full-size candy bars! Holding the bowl out to the boys, he instructs them to each take one candy bar of their choice. As this is occurring, Mooch swears he's seeing a glorious glowing light, like a shimmering halo, behind Mr. Anchor's head. *He's a Candy Angel!*

The offered candy bar selection is: Kit Kat (Mike—his favorite), Hershey's (Mooch—all chocolate), Snickers (Phil—salty and sweet), 3 Musketeers (Cruz—the largest), and Milky Way. They all thank Mr. Anchor before heading toward the driveway, ecstatic with what they've just received.

As they leave the porch, Mike turns to Cruz and says, "I thought Snickers was your favorite candy bar?"

"Yeah, I guess it is, but the 3 Musketeers was bigger—had to go with quantity."

Now out of view from Mr. Anchor, Mooch and Phil huddle close to the far end of the garage door, turning their backs to approaching trick-or-treaters. Out of their backpacks, they pull thin black capes and cheap rubber, slicked-back, vampire hair wigs. They put the vampire gear on over their main costumes, followed by the finishing touch—the vampire teeth obtained earlier at the Krisyzniaks' house. After placing the teeth in their mouths, they take a couple of quick practice "smacks" with their jaws and then turn to return to the front porch for another go.

Mike and Cruz stay behind. They don't approve of and refuse to take any part in this clear violation of the Trick-or-Treating Code. Mooch and Phil vanish around the corner of the garage on their way to the porch.

Half joking and half serious, Mike yells, "Crooks!"

For Mooch this minuscule and highly debatable breach of the Trick-or-Treating Code is justified. For him it is all about the candy (in particular the chocolate). Who better to dispose of such scrumptious delicacies than he?

For Phil the notion that their actions are a breach of the Trick-or-Treating Code is merely a technicality raised by those who interpret the code literally. He chooses to interpret the code as guidelines more than rules, at least in this case. For Phil, it's all about perfectly executing a masterful plan—a challenge he simply can't resist.

Waiting on the driveway, Mike and Cruz figure it's probably a fifty-fifty proposition Mooch and Phil will succeed. They'll either deceive Mr. Anchor and covertly obtain another full-size candy bar, or they'll get caught red-handed and risk having the first bars confiscated. With the suspense growing, they impatiently wait. After a few more moments, Phil and Mooch finally appear from around the corner and raise their arms into the air!

"Score!" exclaims Phil, removing his vampire teeth from his mouth as Mooch leaps (as much as Mooch can "leap") with excitement.

Cruz just shakes his head, smiling in disbelief.

"Nice work, Johnny Dangerously," says Mike, alluding to the comedic gangster film starring Michael Keaton that they all enjoy.

Mooch kisses his second Hershey's bar and raises it to the sky with both hands, ceremoniously proclaiming, "Magnificent! Thank you!"

Phil and Mooch high-five each other and then remove their vampire teeth, wigs, and capes and place them in their backpacks. Phil does so neatly while Mooch crumples and stuffs.

As the gang heads to the next stop, Phil and Mooch reenact for the other two their vampire caper on the Anchors' porch, generating laughs all around.

15

The Packers'

Hoping for what they've been calling the potential *jackpot of all jack-pots*, the gang runs as fast as they can to the Packers' house. Their expectations for this house are heightened after the intel obtained by Mike a couple mornings ago while sitting at his kitchen table eating breakfast before school. He overheard part of a telephone conversation between his mom and one of her good friends, Mrs. Packer. Based on what Mike gleaned from the half of the conversation he could hear, Mr. Packer was apparently given a large quantity of full-size bags of M&M's—not the Halloween-candy size, the family size!

You see, Mr. Packer is the general manager at the candy wholesaler in town. A while back his company mistakenly received an extra box of M&M's—a box the manufacturer didn't require be returned. This extra box has been sitting in the warehouse for quite some time and was recently rediscovered by Mr. Packer. Nearing the expiration date, per company policy, the wholesaler can't keep it any longer and so, headquarters gave permission to Mr. Packer to distribute the candy as he chooses. Being a generous man, he gave half the bags to key employees, but has allegedly kept half to give away to some very lucky trick-or-treaters on Halloween!

Mike's mom was sworn to secrecy as the Packers don't want a mob of kids rushing their front door given the limited supply. She doesn't know Mike overheard the conversation, and Mike hasn't told anyone except the other members of his gang.

Based on this intel, the Packers' house arguably should've been the first major house visited, but considering the manner in which the intel was obtained, the gang couldn't be 100 percent sure of its reliability. Thus, they elected to go for the "sure thing" Anchor house first. But now the timing is right and the gang must get to the Packers' quickly to ensure they have a chance to obtain the alleged large bags of M&M's that will presumably be distributed on a first-come, first-served basis.

They arrive at the end of the driveway and take a moment to catch their breaths from the sprint they just completed. As they stand on the sidewalk, the foursome stares at the house with great expectations. Enthusiastically they proceed forward.

"Keep your fingers and toes crossed, boys," states Mike in a hopeful voice as they turn the corner around the garage, the porch now in full sight.

"Oh, Mikey! This is going to be good! I can sense it!" says Mooch excitedly, hardly able to contain himself as drool literally drips from his mouth.

"Please have what we think you have, please have what we think you have, please have what we think you have . . . ," recites Phil as he approaches the front door.

Mike rings the doorbell. *Ding-dong.* The anticipation growing with every second, the gang is as excited and hopeful as they can ever remember, their hearts almost beating out of their chests. For what seems an eternity, they wait on the doorstep for a sound, a motion, anything signaling a presence from within the house. With no sign of anything or anyone inside, Mike decides to ring the doorbell again. As his finger nears the button a rustling is heard from inside, followed by faint voices.

"George! Kids at the front door!"

"I hear it, Martha. I'm getting it."

The door opens slowly to reveal Mr. Packer standing in the foyer.

"TRICK-OR-TREAT!" yell the boys (Mooch wiping the drool from his mouth as he yells).

"Well hello there, boys . . . You're in luck tonight! We have a special treat for you!" replies Mr. Packer, his excitement nearly equaling that of the boys.

He then reaches behind the door and pulls forward a box full of none other than, you guessed it, FULL-SIZED bags of M&M's. Jackpot! Seeing this, Mooch nearly faints, overcome in the moment, and Phil is speechless as he stares at the box, unable to move.

"Regular or peanut?" asks Mr. Packer.

Mooch and Mike go for regular, and Phil and Cruz select peanut. They receive their bags ceremoniously with open hands and subsequently handle them with great care, as if they're receiving fragile works of art.

"Thanks! Thanks a bunch, Mr. Packer!" they exclaim together as they all look upon the bags and then back up, in awe, at yet another Candy Angel.

"You're very welcome, boys. Enjoy. Your timing was impeccable. We have a limited supply; they won't last much longer," replies Mr. Packer looking upon the boys with a twinkle of pride in his eyes, knowing he just made their night.

As they turn to walk away, Mrs. Packer, one of the nicest ladies in the neighborhood, walks up behind her husband and waves good-bye to the boys. They wave back and thank her as well. Turning the corner around the garage, now walking down the driveway, they turn to each other.

"WHOO! HOO!" they scream, jumping up in the air and pumping their fists to the sky.

"I love it when a plan comes together!" states Phil.

"Way to go, Mikey! That was awesome! What a score!" exclaims Mooch.

Walking away, they feel as if a divine light is illuminating their path and can't help but think to themselves that tonight the Candy Gods are truly with them.

"I feel like a real archeologist who just discovered the mother lode!" states Phil.

"Or a baseball player who just hit a walk-off homer in Game 7 of the World Series!" adds Mooch.

"A basketball player who just made the winning bucket at the buzzer, Game 7 of the NBA Finals!" says Mike.

After a round of well-earned high fives and another loud collective cheer, they walk triumphantly to the next house.

16

The Gullys'

The gang is relatively certain the Gullys won't be home. That's been the case for the last three or four years. And so, they're guessing the Gullys will leave their traditional large bowl of candy on the porch with a sign reading "Please Take Only One Piece Each. Happy Halloween!"

"Okay, Mooch. We need to lay down the ground rules now before you get caught up in another situation where you can't control yourself and it turns into another mega scene," states Mike as they walk up the Gullys' driveway.

Two years ago, at this very house, Mooch committed an undeniably egregious breach of the Trick-or-Treating Code—his greed for candy getting the best of him. It was a breach Mooch willingly acknowledges and one the others will never let him forget.

"Yeah, yeah. I know. I know," replies Mooch, attempting to downplay the situation, tired of hearing about it once again. "It was embarrassing enough then. You guys don't have to remind me of it every single day, do you?"

"Yeah, we do," replies Phil as Mike and Cruz laugh.

Flashback to Halloween Two Years Ago

"Please take only one piece each. Happy Halloween!" narrates Phil as he and the others stand on the Gullys' porch, reading the sign placed above a large bowl of candy resting on a lawn chair.

The sign is a large piece of orange construction paper with black Halloween-gothic, cobweb-covered letters glued to it, arranged in an undulating pattern. The lawn chair is of black, orange, and white striping—very "Halloween-ish."

"Jackpot!" exclaims Mooch. "A humungous bowl jammed full of chocolate bars, and it's all ours for the taking!"

He purposefully places his bag on the ground, crouches down, and grabs the bowl with his arms straddling each side, and motions to the others to assist in his thievery.

"Mikey, open your bag. Quick. I'll pour some in each of our bags."

"No, Mooch. NO!" yells Cruz.

"Yeah, that would be a humungous violation of the Trick-or-Treating Code. We can't," agrees Mike.

"Come on, guys! A *huge* bowl chock-full of scrumptious chocolate bars! This is *the* opportunity of a lifetime. We have to seize the moment, get it while it's hot!" pleads Mooch.

Phil remains silent on the matter, still calculating whether or not this would technically be considered a breach of the TOT code.

"No, we can't. As a compromise, we can take two pieces each. The rest is to be left for others," demands Mike.

In anger, Cruz abruptly picks Mooch's bag up off the ground and shoves it forcefully into his belly. Upon impact, Mooch bends over at the waist and drops down on one knee in pain. Gasping to catch his breath, he places one hand on the side of the house to prevent himself from completely collapsing. After taking a couple seconds to gather himself, he looks up at Cruz to shout at him, but quickly thinks better of it with Cruz glaring down at him in fierce disapproval.

First Mike, then Cruz, and then Phil (hesitantly—still not decided on the matter) take two pieces each of candy and throw them into their bags.

Mooch slowly rises to his feet, still gasping for air. With Cruz watching his every move, he slowly takes two pieces for himself and tosses them into his bag. He slants a look at the others—partially ashamed of what he attempted to do and partially angry that he wasn't able to accomplish his goal.

The others watch him intently for a few moments to ensure he doesn't have a relapse and make another attempt at the candy bowl.

Sensing their surveillance, Mooch turns away and steps off the porch. The others follow. As they reach the midpoint of the driveway, the trio passes the plodding Mooch, leaving him to bring up the rear.

"Crisis averted," says Phil, chuckling.

"Yeah, pretty proud of you, buddy, for maintaining self-restraint," commends Mike, believing they are now in the clear.

But Mooch, now boiling over with desire, is no longer able to contain himself and abruptly stops, turns, and propels himself back toward the Gullys' porch.

"No!" yells Mike. "Stop!"

"Uh-oh," remarks Phil.

Mike and Cruz simultaneously chase Mooch. But given his head start and uncontrollable craving, Mooch reaches the porch first. He quickly grabs the bowl with one hand while holding his bag open with the other. With the intent of pouring the entire contents into his bag, he commences tipping the bowl. Before candy can reach the brim of the bowl, in one continuous motion, Mike grabs the low point of the bowl, tilts it upward, and pulls it toward him. Cruz subsequently grabs Mooch with both arms around his waist and begins to pull him backward away from Mike and the bowl. Mooch struggles with all his might to fight off Cruz, but he can't match Cruz's strength. Mooch's hand begins to separate from the bowl, his fingers straightening and losing their grip. In a last act of desperation, Mooch releases his bag and uses the hand that was holding it to grab the bowl, allowing him to now grasp it with both hands.

"Argh. Mine!" yells Mooch as he struggles against Mike in front of him and Cruz behind him.

Mike matches Mooch's move, placing both his hands on the bowl, and pulls it forcefully toward him with all he has, commencing a tug of war.

SNAP! Mooch loses his grip and instantly all three fall to the ground—Mike in one direction with the jiggling bowl in tow, pieces of candy trickling out the sides, and Mooch and Cruz in the other direction, empty-handed. Upon impact, Mike's elbow hits the ground, forcing his arm to straighten and extend outward. The contents of the bowl launch into the air and ultimately splash to the ground.

They sit up, gather themselves, and look around to see candy scattered everywhere. They then look at each other as if to say, *Oh, no!*

Phil can't believe what he has witnessed. In a panic, fearful that someone may have seen or will soon see what happened, he yells, "Let's go! NOW!"

Mike and Cruz spring to their feet, grab their bags, and begin to run. Mooch more slowly gathers himself, rises, grabs his bag, and begins to "run," but slows for brief moments along the way to "inconspicuously" scoop pieces of candy off the ground.

"What the heck was that?!" an aggravated Mike asks Mooch as they reach the sidewalk.

Mooch just shrugs his shoulders and says, "I don't know. I just *couldn't* resist."

"You made a huge mess. That *will not* happen again!" proclaims Mike as he grabs his elbow and begins rubbing it in pain. "Argh, that hurts."

"Sorry, Mikey," says Mooch sheepishly. "Okay. Okay. Never again."

Back to Halloween This Year

"We don't need another incident like we had two years ago. Got it, Mooch?" commands Cruz.

"Okay, okay. But look at that: a mega-size bowl overflowing with delicious candy. I'm thinking we should take *four* pieces each. There will still be plenty for everyone else," suggests Mooch, licking his lips as Phil nods in agreement.

"*Three* each, exactly. No more, no less. Deal?" compromises Mike.

Cruz prefers they only take the two pieces (as originally decided two years ago). But he knows Mike's suggestion should sufficiently appease Mooch and avoid another meltdown. So, he reluctantly agrees.

Phil and Mooch nod their heads in agreement as they each calmly take three pieces—selecting the best pieces, of course—and happily toss them into their bags.

As they turn to walk away, the others watching intently, see Mooch "covertly" snag a fourth piece. He just can't resist. Mike and Cruz chuckle and shake their heads in disbelief. They can't help but respect Mooch's consistency and persistence.

Mooch remains frozen, standing over the bowl staring down in awe at all the remaining candy. The thought of grabbing the entire bowl and pouring it into his bag begins to trickle into his mind. He licks his lips in anticipation. He begins to reach back into the bowl. Without hesitation, Cruz grabs his arm and abruptly pulls him away, dragging him off the porch and down the driveway. Mooch gazes back at the bowl heartbroken, thinking about what might have been.

17

Girl Gang

The gang works their way through another group of minor houses, gathering what they consider to be better-than-average candy. Still on top of the world from successful gatherings at the Anchors' and Packers' houses, they're having the time of their lives, cracking jokes, eating candy, and taking in all that is the amazing splendor of Halloween. Along the way they see Curtis Brath and his group—a group they've dubbed the Parental Control Pack because they're always escorted by their parents while trick-or-treating.

"Poor Brath. How awful would that be?" empathizes Mooch.

"I know. Having your parents stalking you the entire route would be horrible. I'd rather just stay home and save the embarrassment," says Phil.

"Yeah, I feel bad for those guys too," adds Mike.

"Well, I don't know about the staying-home part. I would *have* to venture out and collect all these delicious sweet treats, no matter how grim the circumstances," clarifies Mooch.

Chuckling, Phil replies, "Yeah, the embarrassment would probably be worth it—can't stay home on the greatest night of the year."

"Hopefully they don't run into Josh and his crew. He'll eat those guys alive," states Mike.

"Having their parents close will save them from Pealy. He *never* shows his true colors in front of adults," counters Phil as Mike nods in agreement.

"Ain't that the truth. He's as sneaky as he is evil," adds Mooch. "*Pealy!*"

They turn the corner to head toward the next major house and see Lisa, Roni, and Terry walking toward them. The gang members instantly transform their demeanor from roughhousing and joking to calm and cool. Girls are present, no time for nonsense.

Lisa is dressed as Catwoman, Roni as a Dallas Cowboys cheerleader, and Terry as Madonna. As they approach, Mike is surprised Lisa isn't in a Wonder Woman costume. *She looks amazing. I should've gone trick-or-treating with her.* Then he turns back to look at Mooch and is reminded why he didn't. He couldn't let his best friend down, not on his farewell tour. *Catwoman?! Why is she Catwoman?!* he wonders. She must have changed her mind after he told her he couldn't go with her. He concludes he can't really blame her for that.

"Hey, boys. Happy Halloween. What's up?" asks Lisa with an uncharacteristic air of indifference.

"Not much," replies Mike. "What're you up to?"

"Just trick-or-treating," states Lisa, intentionally looking at everyone but Mike.

"Getting lots of good candy?" asks Mike as he attempts to make eye contact with Lisa.

"Lots of 'purr-fect' candy," Lisa says, scratching her hand in the air like a cat and still refusing to look at Mike.

"Ha! Catwoman. 'Purr-fect.' I get it!" says Mooch as the others laugh as well.

"Yes, we've 'scored' big so far!" adds Roni as she makes a couple of cheerleading moves.

"Nice football costume, Smoochy," blurts Terry.

"It's not a football costume. It's a baseball costume. I'm Babe Ru—"

"I know, Smooch. You're Baby Ruth. I was just kidding."

Feeling a little embarrassed, Mooch decides to ignore her misunderstanding and attempts to redeem himself, "I like your Madonna cost—"

"Look, we have Catwoman and Superman! Aren't you guys like arch-rivals or something?" asks Terry condescendingly to Mike.

Irritated that Terry cut him off twice, Mooch responds in Mike's defense. "No. Superman and Catwoman don't fight. They're in diff—"

"Wouldn't be a fair fight anyway. Catwoman would definitely win," blurts Terry.

This triggers resounding disagreement from the gang, who laugh loudly at this egregiously incorrect statement.

Phil and Mooch banter back and forth about how easy it would be for Superman to destroy Catwoman and how it wouldn't even be *remotely close*, in any way, to a contest. No one in their right mind would think such a thing, they conclude.

"And I'm not BABY Ruth, the candy bar. I'm BABE Ruth, the baseball—"

"Catwoman's weapon isn't strength, boys," interrupts Lisa, who's growing tired of this apparently endless chatter. "Catwoman doesn't have to fight to win. She has other, much more effective, methods at her disposal."

"That's right. And she favors Batman over Superman—by a mile," states a voice walking up from behind the girls.

Recognizing this voice of evil, the gang looks beyond the girls to see Josh Pealy joining the group. He's dressed as Batman! Beside him are Bobby Poda dressed as a vampire from *The Lost Boys*, Rob Broadway as the recently retired star running back for the Chicago Bears, Walter Payton, and Travis Bennett as Mario (from the *Super Mario Bros.* video game).

"Oh boy, it's Pealy and his crew of goons. Hooray!" says Mooch sarcastically. "Our 'temporary' vampire costumes are better than his," he whispers to Phil referring to Bobby's costume.

"Oh boy, it's the Moocher dressed as John Kruk. How original. Only costume that would fit?" asks Bobby referring to Mooch's likeness to the famous overweight Philadelphia Phillies baseball star.

"Shut up, Count Chocula. I'm not John Kruk, I'm Babe—"

"At least we're not trick-or-treating with Donkey Kong," says Phil, pointing at Travis and laughing. "Do you smash each piece of candy before eating?"

"I'm not Donkey Kong. I'm Mar—"

"Careful, 'Archeology Boy,' I'll take your whip and use it to snag your bag of candy away from you," says Bobby staring at Phil.

"Try it," replies Cruz, staring Bobby down.

"Hey, Superman, why don't you just huddle up your gang and fly away? The girls are trick-or-treating with us tonight," says Josh to Mike.

Crushed by this news, Mike's face drops. *She's trick-or-treating with Josh Pealy?! Josh-the-dirt-bag-scumbag Pealy?! Really?! How could this be? Doesn't she realize how evil and awful he is? What is happening?!*

"Ha! Whatever, Bat Boy. I think you sniffed too much of that hallucination gas from your utility belt," says Mooch with a laugh of disbelief.

"Come on, guys. Let's go. We've heard enough nonsense for tonight," says Lisa as she walks away, gesturing to her friends, Josh, and his crew to follow.

Lisa waits for Josh to catch up, and they walk away together. Not holding hands, but close to each other—signifying that they are, in fact, trick-or-treating together.

Mike is flabbergasted, completely deflated, entirely crushed. Lisa has betrayed him in the worst way possible.

Mooch is equally disheartened as he watches Terry and Bobby walking and talking together behind Lisa and Josh. *Josh and his crew got the best of us AGAIN. This is so unfair!*

Seeing that Mike is heartbroken, Phil and Cruz tug on his arm and convince him to press on. There's still a lot of the TOTR left. No time to waste. As they head to the next house, Mooch remains motionless, still staring at the enemy strolling away with the girls.

"Snap out of it, Smooch! There's work to be done," says Phil as he slaps Mooch on the face.

"Ow!"

Before he commits to moving on, Mike takes one last look at Lisa and catches her glancing back at him. A sense of relief rushes over him. *Maybe things with Lisa aren't as dire as they seem. Maybe she's trick-or-treating with Josh to get back at me for bailing on her.* That's a good sign—if she's upset with him, she still likes him. And there's just no way she'd actually want to go with Josh. *No way.* He's confident they'll see each other before the night is over and hopes that interaction between them will be different, better.

Rubbing his face after getting slapped by Phil, Mooch's eyes remain locked on Josh's Crew and the girls as they disappear into the darkness. Deciding he's seen enough, he begins to look away but then stops abruptly, seeing Terry whisper something into Bobby's ear—something that has Bobby noticeably interested.

"Come on, buddy. Phil's right, we have to forget about those guys. Let's go get some more candy—some awesome candy," Mike encourages Mooch as he gives him a pat on the back and points him in the direction the others are headed.

18

Parental Control Pack

Curtis Brath is lumbering along his trick-or-treating path in typical form, with his parents in tow. His two friends, Thomas Zalezny and Sebastian Deeble, are plodding along beside him with their parents following closely behind. These three form the Parental Control Pack (PC Pack for short)—a name coined by Mooch. They walk sheepishly with their heads down to avoid making eye contact with other groups of kids. There's nothing more embarrassing for an eleven-year-old boy on Halloween night than being escorted by your mom and dad door to door in your own neighborhood. Desperate to separate themselves from their parents, even if only for brief moments, the PC Pack seeks out opportunities to gain independence every step of the way. With these opportunities, however, comes the risk of spotlighting their embarrassing situation as their parents yell out to them to slow down or return to the group. Thus, such opportunities are often pondered, but rarely attempted.

The parents, both moms and dads, trail behind like a pack of stalking coyotes, watching every move and barking at any sign of disobedience. Fixated solely on what their boys are doing, and lacking the social skills necessary to carry on a conversation, they walk in silence. Adding insult to injury, the parents regulate candy intake along the way, refusing to let the boys taste the fruits of their labor until they return home. So restrictive are their parents, this year the boys almost chose to stay home for the night.

Lifting his head (as he does periodically to survey who's in the area), Curtis spots Josh Pealy and his crew about fifty yards ahead. Panicked, not wanting Josh to see him, Curtis quickly lowers his head, stops, and turns to address his dad.

"Maybe we should head back that way?" he says, pointing in the direction opposite from where Josh is approaching.

"Why would we do that? We still have five more houses on this side of the street, and then we'll cross over and go to the houses on the other side of the street, like we always do," replies Mrs. Brath, answering for her husband, as she always does.

Slogging along with their heads down and unaware of the conversation between Curtis and his parents, Sebastian and Thomas continue on toward the next house, getting closer and closer to Josh. Josh and his crew are focused on Lisa and her friends, so they haven't yet spotted Curtis and his friends.

"I just think the candy will be better if we head that way. *Please?!*" implores Curtis to his parents.

Recognizing the panic in Curtis's voice, his friends raise their heads inquisitively to see what all the fuss is about. As they do, they spot Josh and his crew just ahead and become equally alarmed.

"Yeah, maybe we should turn around. I'm getting kind of tired," says Sebastian, turning his back to the approaching group as Thomas frantically nods his head in emphatic agreement.

"Sebastian Patrick, how could you possibly be tired already? It's Halloween night! This fun only comes once a year. Let's keep moving— you'll get your second wind," states Mrs. Deeble as the other hovering parents nod in collective concurrence.

"But, Mom—"

"That's enough, son. Mind your mother," orders Mr. Deeble, cutting off Sebastian before he can complete his plea.

Defeated, the three boys lower their heads and stand still, huddled together with their backs toward Josh's group, hoping not to be spotted. Still engulfed in their conversation with the girls, Josh and his crew completely ignore Curtis and his friends, walking right by them. As they follow the others to the porch, the three boys are relieved at not having to face the insults they feared but are equally disappointed that they weren't even noticed.

"Can you believe that? Eleven years old and still trick-or-treating with your parents!" says Josh, peeking back at Curtis and his friends.

"I know! Deeble and company never disappoint! I bet their parents picked out their costumes too," scoffs Bobby Poda.

"Ha! Yeah! They probably have to ask permission before eating a piece of candy," joins in Travis Bennett.

Having passed the corner of the garage, now out of the waiting parents' sight, Josh stops and turns to face the three boys. Exaggerating Sebastian's name as he often does, he whispers with a big smile, "Hey, SEE-BASS-TEE-ANN, when you get back to your mommy, don't let go of her hand—it's dangerous out there!"

"My name is Patrick!" replies Sebastian, visibly irritated. While his given first name is Sebastian and that's what his parents call him, he hates it and prefers to be called Patrick.

"Hey, SEE-BASS-TEE-ANN, make sure your mommy checks each piece of candy thoroughly before eating—there are all kinds of weirdos out here!" says Bobby as the entire crew giggles.

"Get up there and get me some candy," says Josh as he glares into the Curtis's eyes.

All their dignity seemingly lost, the three boys slouch toward the porch, obtain the candy offered, return to Josh, and hand it to him.

"Oh no. I need more than that. One *handful* each—in my bag!" demands Josh, holding his bag open and pushing it toward them.

"Josh, don't you think that's a little much?" asks Lisa, shocked by his request.

"Well, Curtis and his friends already promised us they would give us some of their candy. They made a deal earlier. Isn't that true, Curty-Boy?" replies Josh, lying.

Knowing he must agree or face a much worse fate at another time, Curtis bows his head in acceptance. Each of the three boys slowly reaches into his bag, grabs a handful of candy, and throw it into the crew's bags—one into Josh's, one into Bobby's, and one into Travis's.

"You forgot one," says Josh, referring to Rob, as he looks at Sebastian.

"I'm good," says Rob, not wanting to push the issue any further, sensing that may send the girls over the edge.

Josh looks at Rob with mild disgust and turns toward the PC Pack to give them one last glare. He closes his bag and barges in between Curtis and Sebastian, nearly knocking them to the ground, as he heads toward the porch. The other crew members follow Josh's path, also knocking into the boys and laughing as they wave good-bye.

Turning back to face Curtis, Josh scoffs, "Hey, youngsters, be sure to look both ways before crossing the street and be sure to get home before it gets dark!"

Dejected, the trio walks away from the porch toward the driveway. Lisa and Roni give them sympathetic looks as they pass.

"You guys shouldn't treat them like that. They didn't do anything to deserve that," states Lisa.

"Yeah, that was just mean. Not cool," adds Roni.

"They had it coming," replies Bobby as Josh nods in agreement.

"Why the long faces, boys?" asks Mrs. Brath as the deflated trio returns to the sidewalk.

Curtis, Thomas, and Sebastian remain silent and just shrug their shoulders—not wanting to recount the embarrassment of what just occurred and fearing what Josh would do if he found out they told on him.

"Did something happen on the porch with those boys and girls? Did they do something mean to you?" inquires Mrs. Brath. "Curtis?"

"No, Mom. Nothing happened. It's fine."

"Well, I wouldn't think so. Josh Pealy has always been such a nice, respectful young man. But you never know; anyone is susceptible to dishonesty without parental supervision. That's why we're here with you boys. To keep you out of trouble, and to keep trouble away," says Mrs. Deeble as the other parents nod in agreement.

In a last-ditch effort to salvage some dignity by obtaining a sliver of freedom, Curtis turns to his dad and says, "Dad, we're fine. We won't get into trouble and trouble won't find us. We can take care of ourselves. How about we go off on our own for the rest of the way?"

"Oh, I don't think we can allow that, sweetie. It's just too dangerous these days. Besides, we're having so much fun. Wouldn't want to spoil it now," replies Mrs. Brath, with the other parents bobbing their heads again in agreement.

Completely dejected and entirely defeated, the three boys forge ahead with heads hanging at a new low and parents in tow.

19

New "Rich" Neighbors

The inhabitants of what they hope will be the next major house are new to the neighborhood, having just moved in last month. The gang is excited. The rumor circulating around school is that this new family is rich, which most likely means great candy and lots of it.

In eager anticipation, Mooch dreams out loud about the amazing candy they may pass out. "Perhaps it will be *giant* Hershey's Kisses? No, better—giant *bags* of Hershey's Kisses! So big they'll fill up our backpacks!"

"Yeah! I heard at their old house they actually used a shovel to dump the candy into the kids' Halloween bags!" exclaims Phil.

"What do you think they'll give us, Mikey?" asks Mooch.

"I think it'll be good, but I don't think the shovel story is true," responds Mike.

"Yeah, probably too good to be true, but still fun to dream about. You never know," states Phil.

As they approach the house, the lights are on—a good sign. Mooch rings the doorbell, pressing hard and long to ensure it rings. Hearing the welcoming *ding-dong* echo inside the house, they wait breathlessly as they stare impatiently at the door. After a few seconds, no one answers—no sound is heard and no motion is detected. They look at each other in disappointment—Mooch with an expression more like frustration on his face.

"Maybe they didn't hear it," says Phil as Mooch shakes his head in hopeful agreement.

Mooch rings the doorbell again, even more deliberately than the last time, and they wait again, with now tempered anticipation. Still no sound or movement comes from inside the house.

"Something must be wrong! Maybe they're in the basement and can't hear the doorbell, or maybe they're old and—"

"Let me try it," says Mike as he rings the doorbell in a firm, swift motion.

They all stand motionless and silent, carefully listening so as to again confirm the doorbell's *ding-dong* inside the house—it's working. They wait longer this time, listening for any peep, looking for any movement. Nothing.

With Mooch now pacing back and forth in frustration and Phil attempting to peer through a small crack in the drapes inside the narrow window next to the door, Mike decides they've waited long enough and announces, "Well, looks like no one's home. Let's roll."

"NO!" shouts Mooch, refusing to give up. "And give up on the mother lode?!"

"They *have* to be home! How can you *not* be home on Halloween night—it's an outrage!" agrees Phil, grabbing Mike's arm to prevent him from turning away from the door.

"Guys, we're wasting time. They're not home, and we have to go to stay on schedule," argues Mike.

"Ugh," mutters Phil, "who leaves their porch lights on, on Halloween night, and then ISN'T home? Or, who sits in an area of the house where you can't hear the doorbell or refuses to answer the door?! Not cool!"

"If you're not going to be home, the decent thing to do is at least leave out a bowl. It's standard Halloween etiquette!" says Mooch swinging his bag around, gesturing as if to hit the house with it. "Happy HallAWAY!"

"So much potential, so disappointing. Cross that one off the TOTR," complains Phil.

They turn away from the porch and head down the concrete path past the corner of the garage and then down the driveway. Mooch and Phil take another look back at the house, hoping for a sudden opening of the front door followed by an epic waterfall-like release of candy. But, to their dismay, there is no such occurrence. As they reach the sidewalk, Josh's Crew approaches, but Lisa and her friends aren't with them. They can be seen in the distance talking with another group of girls.

"Nobody home there, boys—wasted your time—so much for your masterful planning. Why don't you just give us your candy now and save us the trouble of having to take it from you later?" Josh asks as Bobby smiles next to him and Rob and Travis laugh.

As Cruz stares Josh down, Mooch retorts, "Ha! No thanks. How about you open up your bag and I take a dump in it? Just the way you like it."

Mike and Phil laugh, and even Cruz manages a chuckle.

Josh moves so he's face to face, noses nearly touching, with Mooch, "Go for it. You'll be wearing my bag as a hat."

Cruz moves in to separate Josh and Mooch.

"Maybe we should just cut holes in the bottom of your bags like we did two years ago. How much candy did you lose that year?" asks Bobby, laughing.

"A LOT! Ha! Or maybe we already did that, and you morons just haven't noticed yet," says Travis, looking down at the Mooch's bag.

Mooch and Phil laugh this off but take a quick peek down at their bags to verify they don't have holes.

"C'mon, guys. We're just wasting our time with these goons," says Mike, gesturing to move onward.

Josh and his crew stay behind. Unable to pass up any chance to mess with others, they take full advantage of an approaching opportunity—a group of trick-or-treaters coming to the house the gang just left.

Phil has dubbed this group the No-Plan Bunch. They're notoriously *awful* at trick-or-treating. They show up late (after the best candy is gone) or at the wrong time (when Josh and his crew are present to commandeer their candy) to the key houses. And they continue to make the same mistakes year after year.

Flashback to Halloween Last Year

About halfway through the evening, the gang witnesses Jack Palmer, Alex Johnson, and Dylan Jones (a.k.a. the No-Plan Bunch) leaving the Anchors' house (site of the full-size candy bars) empty-handed and angry because the Anchors just ran out of candy—they got there too late!

"Rookies!" Mooch yells at them from across the street.

"Buzz off!" retorts Jack, the self-proclaimed leader of the ten-year-old group.

"Enjoying those full-size candy bars, are yah?!" asks Phil, laughing.

"We were NEVER that bad, not even in our early years. Disgraceful," proclaims Mooch as Phil emphatically nods in agreement.

Despite the teasing from Mike's Gang, Jack and his sidekicks quickly cross the street toward them. As always, they're eager to pick the gang's brains about what they should have done, should do, where they should go next, etc.

"Things not going so well?" asks Mooch.

"Could be better," replies a sheepish Alex.

"Let me guess. You went to the Hotters' first and spent too much time there?" asks Mooch.

"No . . . Well, maybe . . . Okay, yeah. We did," answers Jack as Dylan nods.

"Tell us you at least got to the Gullys' house in time to grab a few pieces before Pealy and his goons got there," inquires Phil.

"Um, well, no. When we got there all the candy was gone. Only a written note was left that read 'Sorry, suckers. Too late. Empty!' Left by Josh, I think," replies Jack.

"You think?" remarks Phil sarcastically.

In addition to continually failing to plan their route, the trio perpetually sports the most pathetic costumes. Every year they wait until the last minute and then scramble to assemble a mishmash of random apparel. A process that always ends badly, and this year is no exception.

Jack is supposedly a cowboy. He's wearing a black top hat from his dad's closet, a pink bandana from his mom's dresser, his Cub Scout vest (with the assorted patches visible), and already disintegrating "chaps" made out of a brown paper bags taped to his jeans. Ridiculous! Even worse is Alex, who has simply draped an old, white bedsheet over his head with two eyeholes cut in—he's a ghost. How unoriginal and lazy can you be?! To make matters worse, he's wearing his heavy, black-framed glasses *over* the sheet along with very conspicuous and unghost-ly red sneakers.

But the clear winner of this year's Most Pathetic Costume award goes to Dylan, who's dressed as a mummy. Absurdly, he's wrapped several layers of toilet paper around white long underwear that covers his torso and extremities. Toilet paper that has now begun to degrade and fall off in response to a light drizzle earlier in the evening. Dylan's pitiful combination of poor planning (not paying attention to the weather forecast) and last-minute scrambling has cost him. He looks like a giant saggy diaper!

Eager to change the subject from their failure at the Gullys' house, the trio begins a desperate barrage of annoying questions. What's your route? Where'd you go first? Where are you going next? Can we tag along? Etc., etc., etc.

Consolidating his response to all the questions, Mike replies, "Look, guys, if you want to maximize your trick-or-treating, you have to start with a plan. You *never* plan. You just wander around aimlessly. And it costs you every year."

The gang steps past the trio to continue on with the TOTR. As they walk away, they're bombarded with more questions.

"Plan? What kind of plan? Will you help us? Can you teach us?"

Ignoring the questions and continuing to walk, Mooch tells his pals, "Those guys will never learn."

"They can't be helped," adds Phil.

"No. Sadly, they cannot," concludes Mike as they press on.

Back to Halloween This Year

"That house right there is handing out the best candy," Josh tells Jack, Alex, and Dylan.

"Really?! Awesome!" replies Jack.

"Yep, but the people who live there are old and don't hear so well, so you have to ring the doorbell a bunch of times," says Josh, struggling to contain his laughter.

"Yeah, we had to ring it at least twenty times," says Bobby.

"Maybe even thirty—hard to keep track," adds Travis.

"Okay. Thanks, guys!" replies the group as they continue on toward the porch of the house.

As they walk away, Mike's Gang can hear Josh and his goons in the distance laughing as they watch the No-Plan Bunch ring the doorbell time after time.

After about the twelfth attempt, the man of the house aggressively swings open the door. "We have NO candy here! STOP ringing the doorbell! *Please leave!*" he yells.

Startled and scared, the bunch scurries off the porch and down the driveway (passing by Josh and his crew).

"And, *you* kids. OFF my driveway!"

"Yes, sir. Sorry, sir," answers Josh, giving his typical "best-behavior" performance.

"Whoa! That's some Halloween spirit for you! Leave it to Pealy to bring out the worst in people," says Mooch.

"Yeah, but if you don't want kids on your porch on Halloween, how about you post a sign saying so? Or how about not leaving your porch light on, or maybe not being home? What the heck?" questions Phil.

"Crazy stuff. Didn't see that coming. Glad we got out of there before all of that," says Mike. The other gang members nod their adamant agreement and turn to continue on.

20

The Bakers'

The gang has arrived at the Bakers' house, infamously known for handing out homemade (yes, *homemade*) candy. Homemade candy that is also known to be downright awful—too sour or too salty or too spicy or too bland or too hard or too chewy or too slimy or too stinky or any combination of these unappetizing traits. As such, few neighborhood kids dare to stop here on Halloween.

One of the challenges associated with the Bakers' house is that they're known for shutting down early due to Mr. Baker needing to rise early each morning for his job. So, any trick-or-treating must be done in the earlier part of the evening, which requires creative route planning. As other groups of kids walk by without giving the Bakers' house a glance, the gang is relishing the challenge.

While they huddle at the end of driveway, Mooch asks, "Okay, who's in?"

Hesitantly, the other three slowly raise their hands—each fearing the peer pressure that would ensue if they didn't.

"So, what's the challenge this year?" inquires Mike.

"I say eat-what-you-get suicide mission, kamikaze style!" suggests Phil.

"I say we go big again. Evens-and-odds duel-off. Winner picks, loser eats," says Mooch. He is referring to the game they frequently play to settle arguments, choose sides, etc. Two competitors each hide a hand behind their backs, extending one to five fingers. Then one of them chooses "evens" or "odds" as they both bring their hidden hand around to reveal their numbers. The total of the fingers held out by each is added up, making an even or an odd number, thus determining the winner of duel. When four competitors are involved, the losers of the first round vie in the final round to determine the ultimate loser.

"Oh, man. Well, if it's going to be duel-off, it has to be *one* share and not *all* shares like last year," says Phil, as he gags reliving the awful memory of last year when he was the one who had to endure eating FOUR pieces (ALL shares) of Mrs. Baker's so-called candy.

"Agreed!" exclaims Mooch.

"Let's vote: every man for himself or evens-and-odds duel-off—one man's share?" Mike prompts.

Carefully weighing the odds in their heads, they take a few seconds to think and then unanimously vote for an evens-and-odds duel-off, loser eats ONE share, figuring that at least you have a three-out-of-four chance of not having to eat a piece.

Mrs. Baker's concoctions aren't so much candy as very un-Halloween-ish combinations of varying amounts of sugar and what she calls "healthy" ingredients, resulting in a mixture gone horribly wrong. Hard candy is already not a favorite of the gang, especially Mooch, but couple it with awful flavors—such as cloves, nutmeg, ginger, and eucalyptus—and you have a recipe for what may be the world's worst "candy." Also, she uses waxed paper as wrappers, often making it virtually impossible to unwrap cleanly without pesky paper remnants sticking to the "candy."

Having settled on the challenge, they meander slowly toward the front door, each thinking: *There's still time. I can still bail.* But each knows the one who caves first will forever be labeled a wimp, a coward.

"Trick-or-treat!"

Mrs. Baker opens the door immediately—she's been watching them approach. She's excited because few visitors have come by for her confectionary masterpieces this evening. She's wearing a dress covered by an apron that extends to the floor. An unpalatable odor wafts from the kitchen. A stench so awful, it has the boys seriously contemplating an abrupt escape.

"Happy Halloween, boys! Been a slow night—we were beginning to think they canceled trick-or-treating this year."

"Yeah, not tonight, unfortunately," mutters Phil under his breath as he thinks, *Maybe canceling trick-or-treating isn't such a bad idea.*

"Well, obviously not! Okay, you boys are a lucky bunch. I spent all day making my *delicious* and *healthy* world-famous candies. I made lots in anticipation of a busy night. And since you're one of the few groups to come by, I'm going to give you extra. You each get three pieces!" says Mrs. Baker as she proudly hands out the candy.

Initially in shock, the gang's emotions quickly transform to horror, wondering what grave mistake have they've made and thinking, *THREE per share?! Oh no!* With the "candy" in hand and half-turning to leave, the boys are halted by Mrs. Baker.

"May I ask a favor of you nice boys?"

The gang looks at each other, unsure how to answer. After a short period of silence, Mike hesitantly replies, "Sure."

"Great! I spent all day making this delicious candy and Fred refuses to try a piece to let me know how it is. Would you boys be so kind as to each try a piece now and give me your honest feedback? It would mean so much."

After another second or two of silence, all looking at one another befuddled and desperately wanting to not answer, they reluctantly but respectfully agree to comply with her request. In what feels like super-slow motion, every millisecond an eternity, Mrs. Baker places one additional piece in each boy's hand.

"One for you. One for you. One for you. And one for you. Okay . . . "

While Mrs. Baker looks on with great anticipation, they each place the first three pieces given into their bags and then slowly (due to the difficulty imposed by the waxed paper) unwrap the "candy." They look at each other in dreadful regret and wonder, *How bad is this going to be?* They also wonder, given the dramatic unanticipated turn of events, if the evens-and-odds duel-off is still on?

Unfortunately for him, Cruz is the first to unwrap his. He slowly raises the piece to his mouth. He's followed by Mike and Phil. Mooch brings up the rear. Anticipating an awful flavor as the "candy" hits their tongues, they use all their might to maintain as normal a face as possible so as not to disrespect or embarrass Mrs. Baker. The flavors flow through their mouths. Cruz takes his medicine like a man, remaining motionless and silent. Mooch nearly gags and has to turn away. Phil covers his mouth to prevent himself from coughing the "candy" out. And Mike winces in agony.

Somehow Mike finds a way to muster some words. "Very good. Thank you, Mrs. Baker."

"Yeah?! You think? Oh, thank you so much, so much! You're very welcome, boys!" Mrs. Baker is elated by Mike's positive response. As she turns away to grab more pieces, she says, "As a special thank-you, I would like to reward you each with a few more pieces."

Definitely not wanting more, they recognize their opening to end this awful and seemingly never-ending situation. Before Mrs. Baker can turn back around, they turn and run as fast as they can off the porch, around the house, and onto the driveway—Mrs. Baker only catches a glimpse of Mooch's backside as he rounds the corner.

Now out of sight they immediately spit out the "candy." Through a dramatic sequence of coughing and hacking, they exclaim, "BLAH! YUCK! GROSS! UGH!"

"I think mine was butt-flavored," says Mooch. "My dog would've liked it."

"Pretty sure mine was week-old sweaty-sock flavored. You would've liked it," says Mike jokingly.

"I don't think there's a word that describes how horrible mine was," mutters Phil. "No one could possibly like it."

Cruz has no time for words, continuing to spit out every minuscule bit of "flavor" from his mouth.

After catching his breath from the excessive coughing, Mooch proceeds to scrape his tongue with the inside of the brim of his baseball cap in an attempt to remove any and all remnants from his mouth. He raises his right arm and says, "I motion for a revote."

"Agreed, revote," Mike immediately responds. "Who's in for evens—actually, I'm just going to say it. Who wants to skip this challenge all together and move on to the next house?"

Even before Mike can finish the last sentence, the others simultaneously proclaim, "Aye!"

"Last time I visit that house," announces Phil.

"Yep," offers Cruz.

"For sure," states Mike.

Mooch nods in agreement as he sadly realizes he'll no longer have that choice due to his impending move.

The gang continues on the TOTR to what they hope will be better experiences.

21

The Pinchers'

Equal in importance to knowing which houses to visit is knowing which houses to avoid. The Pinchers' is a house that should never be visited. They *never* hand out candy and instead, *always* hand out pennies. That's right, pennies! Who wants pennies? Who needs pennies?! Complete waste of time. Accordingly, the TOTR skips this house.

Josh and his crew, however, make a point of visiting the Pinchers' house every year, with the goal of accumulating as many pennies as possible. Because Mrs. Pincher is stingy with her carefully shined pennies (exactly three to each kid), this year they've made special provisions to accomplish their goal. They've made gloves with magnets attached to the palms, and they plan to wave them over the bowl to collect extra pennies. These gloves use industrial-strength magnets confiscated from Travis's basement. Such items are commonplace at his house, his dad being an electrical engineer who frequently works on home experiments and inventions.

This level of preparation may seem excessive, but it's born from past experience. Last year they attempted to sneak handfuls of pennies from the bowl while Travis distracted Mrs. Pincher. But the plan backfired when her keen sense of touch detected vibrations in the bowl, prompting her to quickly turn around and catch Bobby red-handed. While Bobby was forced to embarrassingly relinquish his handful, Josh and Rob had already swiftly emptied theirs back into the bowl. Thankfully, Mrs. Pincher can't see very well and her memory isn't sharp, so her chances of remembering Bobby this year are low.

They approach the porch and Travis, with mischievous anticipation, rings the doorbell. *Ding-dong.*

"Trick-or-treat!"

"Well hello, boys. Having a fun time this year, are we?"

"Yes, we are, ma'am. Thank you for asking," replies Josh, again in his best-behavior voice.

"Here you go, boys. Don't spend it all in one place," Mrs. Pincher advises while methodically dropping trios of pennies, one at a time, into each of their bags.

As she gets about halfway through the process, Travis jumps into action. "That's an enormous piggy bank you have there." He points to the item resting on the hutch against the wall directly behind the front door.

"Why, yes, it is," she says, turning around to admire it. "My grandmother bought it for me when I was a little girl. You know, some of the money in it is many years—well, decades—old. Technically, it's a 'hog bank,' because it takes the form of a large farm hog . . . "

As Mrs. Pincher rambles about her piggy-hog bank with her back to them, Josh, Bobby, and Rob take advantage of the opening and repeatedly wave their hands over the bowl, accumulating pennies and then dumping them into their bags as quickly as possible. With the magnets working to perfection, they transfer MEGA quantities of pennies in no time at all. And this time Mrs. Pincher doesn't sense a thing.

Having gathered a sufficient number of pennies, Josh cuts off Mrs. Pincher's rambling, "It is a wonderful hog bank, ma'am. Thank you so much for the pennies. We promise we'll put them to very good use. Now, we must be going."

"Oh, yes . . . Of course, boys. You're very welcome. Enjoy the rest of your holiday!" she responds, turning back around to face them, oblivious to the caper the boys just pulled.

Leaving the Pinchers' house, glowing with the success of an ingenious theft, the crew moves on to the second stage of their sinister plan. They must now find Federico Mocha, a new student at their school. He's been in the United States for less than a month now and speaks broken English, still having a lot to learn about the language as well as

American culture and customs. But, most importantly to Josh, Federico is gullible. Having seen him just a few houses ago, it doesn't take long for them to track him down.

"Hey, Federico!" shouts Josh as he approaches the mild-mannered boy from Italy.

"*Ciao, signor* Josh-ah!"

"Chow, Federico! Hey, we have a great deal for you. I have a whole stack of brand-new shiny pennies. Valuable stuff. Money!" states Josh as he shows Federico the handful of sparkling pennies they collected.

"Wow! *Denaro*, money-ah!"

"Yeah, *denaro*! Since you're such a cool guy and we've come to like you so much over the past month, we wanted to do something nice for you. We'll trade you some of these very valuable pennies for candy. One penny for one piece of chocolate. What do you say?" asks Josh.

"Wow! *Grazie!* So very nice-ah! Okay . . . I will take-ah . . . *dieci!*" replies Federico as he shows ten fingers. He reaches into his bag, retrieves ten pieces of candy, and hands them to Josh.

"Okay. And there you go," says Josh as he receives the candy and offers the pennies. "I tell you what, since this trade made you so happy, I'm going to offer you another trade for five more pieces." Josh holds up five fingers. "But I really can't do any more than that. If you want them, you need to let me know now. They're going fast."

"*Grazie! Sì*—yes-ah," replies Federico as he gathers five more pieces of candy and exchanges them for pennies.

"You scored big, buddy! Congratulations!" says Bobby before he makes a soccer-kicking motion while saying, "Score!" He then gives Federico a hearty pat on the back.

Federico grins and nods.

Having completed their mission, Josh and his goons quickly depart in the opposite direction of where Federico is headed. After a few steps, they stop and Josh divvies up the candy—taking more than his fair share, giving Travis the least.

"I can't believe he fell for it!" says Travis.

"I can. He's as gullible as they come. Easy pickings, almost too easy," replies Josh.

"Like taking candy from a baby," says Bobby as he high-fives Josh.

"Hey, Federico! *Ciao!*" yells Mooch as he and the other gang members approach him.

"*Ciao!* Look-ah! Josh trade me-ah shiny pennies-ah. One-ah piece-ah candy each-ah!" exclaims Federico.

"What?!" replies Mooch.

"Wait a minute. You traded Josh one piece of candy for one penny?" asks Mike.

"*Sì*—yes-ah!"

"How many pieces did you trade?" asks Mike.

"*Quindici*," answers Federico as he flashes five fingers three times signaling fifteen, his excitement dwindling as he interprets Mike's body language, sensing that perhaps it was not such a good trade.

"Oh, man. Pealy strikes again," murmurs Mooch, shaking his head.

Mike apologetically explains to Federico that he's just been taken advantage of by Josh.

Federico lowers his head in shame.

"Sorry, Federico. You're just the latest in Josh Pealy's long line of victims," explains Phil, the frustration evident in his voice.

22

Houses of Disappointment and Surprise

The Dentes'

Mrs. Dente traditionally gives out very good candy every year—assorted mini chocolate bars, sometimes two each! This past year, however, she was hired as the receptionist for a dental office and has turned over a new leaf. She has abandoned sugary sweets and is now handing out toothbrushes and floss—much to the gang's disappointment.

"Happy Halloween, boys! This year we have a wonderful surprise for each of you—a Halloween dental-care packet. Here you go! Now remember, brush your teeth twice a day and floss every day to maintain a healthy, happy smile! And most importantly, stay away from sweets!"

Not believing what they're hearing, or seeing, the boys look on in shock as she methodically places the toothbrushes and floss into their bags. Still not fully comprehending what's occurring, they stare down into their bags to see dental supplies floating unfittingly into a sea of delicious candy. It's as if their bags have been contaminated by a foreign substance. As reality sinks in, the boys slowly raise their heads to look at each other. Seeing the look of pure disappointment on each other's faces, they collectively murmur, "Thank you, Mrs. Dente."

"What in the HECK was THAT!? It's bad enough getting a toothbrush and floss, but then it comes with a lecture?! On Halloween? Really?!" asks Mooch as the gang walks slowly away from the porch.

"Whatever, lady! Happy HalloWEIRDO!" adds Phil.

"Scratch that one off the list," says Mike as they head down the driveway and on to the next house.

The Foots'

The Foots historically don't give out anything to get very excited about on Halloween, but they usually distribute decent candy—like Bottle Caps, SweetTARTS, or Starburst. This year, though, Mrs. Foot is handing out leftover Easter candy! While this is typically considered a tacky and lazy move, her choice of delicious Cadbury Crème Eggs or medium-size milk-chocolate Easter bunnies suits the gang just fine!

"Happy Halloween, young men! Have I got a surprise for you! I just so happened to stumble upon an amazing deal at Kmart—they had all this delicious Easter candy on clearance. I couldn't resist, figuring it would be a nice surprise for the neighborhood kids. Something different than just the same old Halloween candy, right?"

"It sure is! This is great!" remarks Mike as he selects an egg.

Phil and Cruz also choose Cadbury eggs, while Mooch goes for the chocolate Easter bunny, of course.

"Enjoy, boys! Happy Halloween!"

"Thank you, Mrs. Foot!" replies Mooch.

"Score! Happy HallowEASTER!" exclaims Phil as the others laugh.

As they walk away from the porch, Mooch remarks, "Man, I *did not* see *that* coming!" shaking his head side to side in disbelief.

"Nobody could have. It's awesome!" replies Phil, almost skipping along as they head to the next house.

The Rosines'

The Rosines always hand out boxes of Raisinets. While this "candy" could technically be categorized as a fruit, the gang considers it acceptable because it's covered in chocolaty goodness. Raisinets also taste good and provide an unusual combination of softness and chewiness, while not being too sticky. A combination that's hard to pass on and so, the Rosines' house is always on the TOTR.

"Happy HEALTHYween, boys!" exclaims Mrs. Rosine.

The boys look at each other, thinking to themselves, *Has she really stolen our shtick of morphing the H-word?* and subsequently wonder what horrific "surprise" they're in for now.

"I figured this year I'd spice things up a bit and give out something a little healthier than we usually do, but still sweet. You kids get so much candy from other houses. It must be refreshing to get something to invigorate your body. Raisins! Nature's candy!"

Mini boxes of raisins?! Plain, ordinary, standard, boring raisins with nothing sugary covering them at all—*naked* raisins! A tragic and highly disappointing maneuver, painfully similar to the stunt pulled by Mrs. Dente earlier. Since Mrs. Rosine is a close friend of Mrs. Dente, this doesn't come as a complete surprise. But it's still very dissatisfying.

Reacting similarly to their experience at the Dentes' house, the despondent boys watch the raisin boxes tumble into their bags, polluting their precious stocks of scrumptious candy.

"Thank you," responds Mike in monotone as Cruz nods and Mooch and Phil linger speechlessly. Finally, they look up at Mrs. Rosine, smile, and slowly walk away.

"Happy HallowNO-THANKS!" exclaims Mooch as he and the others forge on. Hopefully the next house will provide a better outcome.

The Carbons'

Mrs. Carbon typically hands out decent candy like mini packets of Twizzlers or mini boxes of Dots. Not bad. Thus, her house is always good for a quick stop on the TOTR. But this year she's throwing curveballs at trick-or-treaters unlike any twist ever encountered on Halloween before. She's handing out cans of soda! That's right, *full* cans of soda—five types to choose from!

Mooch is first and grabs a Mountain Dew, Mike a Pepsi, Phil a Dr. Pepper, and Cruz a 7-Up. None of them choose root beer.

"Thanks, Mrs. Carbon!" they exclaim.

"You're more than welcome, boys! Figured you could use a little thirst-quenching refreshment, walking around all evening. It's a hot one this year."

"Yes! This is awesome!" replies Phil.

Wasting no time, Mooch immediately cracks his open and proclaims, "I'm parched!" He then chugs the entire can without pause and follows it with a gigantic belch, emanating from way deep in his belly. Shaking the can vigorously to ensure it's completely empty, he announces, "AHH! That hit the spot!"

The others look at him and laugh, having seen this act several times before.

Mrs. Carbon, however, isn't impressed. "Manners, boys. Manners," she says with a look of disgust.

"Oh. Uh, sorry. Excuse me, Mrs. Carbon. My apologies. I guess I just got a little overexcited," replies Mooch as she inclines her head to accept his apology, but still make her disapproval clear.

The others carefully place their sodas in the cooler compartments of their backpacks as they walk to the next stop on the TOTR.

Walking away from the Carbons' house, Mooch is feeling energized after polishing off an entire can of Mountain Dew. As a byproduct of his performance, he continues to let out loud belches as they walk.

"Mikey, a Hershey's bar for a Kit Kat?" he asks, as is customary around this time of the evening.

"Deal," replies Mike as he begins to search his bag for a Hershey's bar.

"What the . . . I can't find a Kit Kat," states Mooch, frantically shoveling through his bag in search.

"Uh-oh. No trade! No trade!" exclaims Phil, laughing.

"I know I had one. Did you take it?" asks Mooch, looking angrily at Phil.

Phil fires back. "What? Why would I—"

"Let me see," demands Mooch as he grabs at Phil's bag.

Phil counters by pulling back aggressively, commencing a mini tug-of-war. In the back-and-forth, Mooch inadvertently knocks off Phil's glasses. Falling to the ground, the right stem cracks and nearly breaks apart, leaving the glasses held together by only a tiny remaining thread of plastic!

"Uh-oh," murmurs Mooch.

"Oh no!" yells Phil. "Look at what you did!"

"Oh crap! I'm sorry. I didn't mean for that to happen."

"Well, it happened. And, we still have a *long way* to go tonight. Haven't even gotten to the Hotters' house yet," retorts Phil, still angry, but quickly calming down as he switches to problem-solving mode.

Mooch offers to help, "Here, let me see it. I can fix—"

"No, I got it," responds Phil, cutting Mooch off as he dives into full diagnosis mode. "Looks like I'm going have to MacGyver this."

He removes the dental floss received earlier from Mrs. Dente and a wood-stick match from his bag. Carefully, he uses the match as a splint, centering it over the break, and ties it tightly around the stem of his glasses with a knot he learned in Cub Scouts, using nearly the entire spool of floss (just to be sure).

"That should hold it for tonight, I think," he remarks proudly, carefully performing a final inspection of his work.

The others look on, impressed yet again by his ingenuity. Even more than that, they're relieved his glasses are fixed. Without his glasses, Phil would be essentially ineffective for the remainder of the night.

"Who would've thought one of us would actually use the floss?" asks Mike as they all laugh.

"Yeah, ever. Let alone tonight!" says Phil.

"Found it!" exclaims Mooch, having finally located a Kit Kat bar in his bag.

Phil gives Mooch a look that says, *Really?*

"Here you go, butthead," says Mike as he hands the Hershey's bar to Mooch and swiftly snags the Kit Kat from his hand.

Mooch immediately unwraps the chocolate bar, gently places it into his mouth, and proceeds to slowly savor every morsel—a move that causes him to fall behind the others. Having to "run" to catch up, he eventually reaches them and places his arm around Phil's shoulder apologetically. Phil returns the gesture, forgiving his pal once again.

23

The Hotters'

Having covered all the major houses, and others offering good candy in their neighborhood, Mike announces, "It's time, guys! Let's roll!"

"Yes!" replies Mooch.

"Let's do it!" adds Phil.

They immediately begin running toward the Hotters' house—home of Andrea Hotter, daughter of Mrs. Hotter, the hottest mom in the neighborhood! For obvious, non-candy-related reasons (the Hotters not being known for their candy excellence), this house *always* makes the rotation. While just missing the cut as one of the major houses on the TOTR due to its so-so candy distribution, tradition dictates it is visited immediately following completion of all major houses in their neighborhood.

As the gang approaches the Hotters' house, the typical horde of dads and countless boys is seen lingering about. One of the groups is the PC Pack. In a feeble and downright embarrassing attempt to impress Mrs. Hotter, Mr. Deeble is dominating her attention by relentlessly engaging her in his standard annoying and nerdy conversation—conversation Mrs. Hotter is clearly not interested in, but continues to tolerate so as not to insult Mr. Deeble.

The boys walk up the driveway as slowly as possible to maximize the duration in which they get to gaze upon Mrs. Hotter's mesmerizing beauty. This year she's looking particularly spectacular, dressed up as Princess Leia from *Return of the Jedi*—and Princess Leia never looked so good! Reaching the beginning of the sidewalk that connects the driveway to the porch, they must now "swim" the rest of the way though the dense crowd of boys and dads packed tightly together. Finally reaching the porch (a.k.a. the Holy Grail), they linger as long as possible, taking in every square millimeter of her sparkling smile, intoxicating perfume, impeccably styled hair, and scanty outfit perfectly fitted to her magnificent body. After only a few moments they're aggressively forced aside by a new crop of eager trick-or-treaters, and retreat to the comparative calm of the front yard.

Clear of the mob, Phil and Mooch stop, remove their backpacks, and pull out their vampire capes, wigs, and teeth.

Taken by surprise, Mike asks, "What's this?"

"What does it look like?" replies Mooch as he frantically fits his wig onto his head.

"That move again?" continues Mike.

"Yes. We're creating the opportunity for a second look at extreme beauty. Got pushed out of there way too soon. Got to get another Mrs. HOOTER close-up!" yells Phil.

"Happy HOTTERween!" exclaims Mooch. "Plus, an added bonus—another piece of candy!"

"Hmm," says Mike, with a hint of jealousy in his voice.

"If you want, you guys can use 'em after we're done," offers Phil, now completely transformed back into a vampire and ready for round two.

Mike and Cruz look at each other in amazement and then look back at the others before they respond in unison, "Okay."

"Oh. So, you guys suddenly approve of this method now, huh?" says Mooch as he and Phil chuckle.

Mike and Cruz sheepishly nod and smile as Mooch and Phil dive back into the swirling crowd.

After a few minutes, they emerge victorious!

"Well worth it! Wow!" exclaims Phil as he and Mooch exchange a high five.

"Happy HallowLEIA!" yells Mooch.

Now anxious to share in the same amazing experience as their friends, Mike and Cruz demand the vampire costumes be removed immediately. They nearly tear them off Mooch and Phil and put them on as quickly as possible—except the vampire teeth, not wanting to risk getting "cooties."

As they begin to dive back into the crowd, Phil screams, "Wait! You can't go *right now*!"

"Why?" responds Mike.

"You have to wait a little bit. We were *just* up there wearing the *same* costumes!" retorts Phil.

Mike and Cruz look at each other, simultaneously shrug their shoulders, and then Mike responds, "We'll take our chances."

They turn and disappear into the mob.

Upon arrival at the door, Mrs. Hotter takes an extended suspicious look them. *Uh-oh, this may not have been the best idea*, they each think.

"Hmm . . . Haven't you two already been here?"

"Oh, us? No, ma'am," replies Mike nervously.

After pausing another moment to take a longer look at them, she replies, "Hmm. Maybe it was another pair of boys . . . But their costumes were almost identical to yours."

"Popular costumes, I guess," replies Mike, now anxious to just obtain the candy and scram!

"No . . . I remember those wigs. The tag is still on yours and it has a chocolate smudge on the side, just like the boy a moment ago," she continues, pointing at the wig on Cruz's head. *Mooch forgot to remove the tag!*

Irritated by the length of this conversation, the other trick-or-treaters begin pushing and shoving the pair in an attempt to remove them from the porch. Realizing they're inciting a frenzy, and that they're stuck in a no-win situation, Cruz panics and quickly turns around, diving back into the crowd. Mike stands frozen for a moment, contemplating his next move. Then he abruptly turns and follows Cruz, disappearing into the crowd.

"You guys sure took your sweet time up there. Did you take pictures?" jokes Mooch as Mike and Cruz return.

"Yeah, things didn't work out quite like we had hoped," replies Mike.

"Why? What happened? Did you get busted?" asks Phil.

"Yep," responds Cruz.

"Yeah, she recognized us because of *this* tag!" exclaims Mike as he grabs the wig off Cruz's head and throws it at Mooch's torso.

"Whoops. Probably should've removed that, I guess," says Mooch apologetically.

"Probably?!" replies an angered Cruz.

"We were sitting ducks. Had no option but to bolt!" states Mike, starting to chuckle after realizing the comedy in what just happened.

"You guys just turned and ran?!" laughs Mooch.

"Yeah! After she noticed the tag and the chocolate smudge, she wouldn't let it go. We knew we were done. Cruz just froze for a second and then ran—smashing his way through the crowd like the real Terminator," explains Mike. "I was left standing there, frozen, all by myself for what seemed like an eternity. Not knowing what to do, I figured I better run for my life too!"

"Ha! That's hilarious!" says Mooch, laughing out loud.

"Wow! Caught red-handed by Mrs. Hotter. You should be ashamed of yourselves!" says Phil facetiously, now also laughing.

"Yeah. We should've known better than to trust in your crazy idea. The worst part is that we were so scared the whole time, we didn't get to enjoy the view properly," continues Mike as he puts Mooch in a headlock and messes his hair.

"It was worth it," says Cruz, grateful for another brief, albeit chaotic, look at Mrs. Hotter.

Releasing the headlock he has on Mooch, Mike agrees, "It sure was! Happy HOOTERween!"

They all laugh and give each other mega high fives. Mooch and Phil gather up their vampire costumes, quickly store them in their backpacks, and hustle to catch up to Mike and Cruz, who've already started toward the next house for another exciting adventure.

24

The Winnys'

Phil studies the TOTR map he just pulled from his backpack, looks down at his watch, and sighs.

"Okay, guys. If we go now, the timing should be just right."

The timing Phil's referring to comes from the recon information Mooch and Cruz obtained at the grocery store earlier in the week.

"You're sure about what you heard, right?" asks Phil.

"Definitely," replies Mooch as Cruz nods in agreement.

What they claim to have overheard was Mrs. Winny telling another mom she'd already purchased several large family-size bags of Reese's Pieces to hand out on Halloween. Her reason for buying Reese's Pieces is that she feels peanut butter is "healthier" than the other candies. Her reason for buying family-size bags is that she and her husband will only be home for about a ten-minute period in between events they must attend on Halloween night. Given the short amount of time they'll be available to hand out candy, she anticipates the number of trick-or-treaters will be low. Accordingly, she desires to make the limited visits memorable, so she plans to hand out entire large bags of Reese's Pieces to each kid! When asked by the other mom why she was bothering to hand out candy at all given her busy schedule, Mrs. Winny said she feels guilty not participating in making trick-or-treating an enjoyable experience for the youngsters. She feels obligated to do her part, however short-lived it may be.

This piece of "juicy" information gathered by Mooch and Cruz is what they're all hoping will be a Junior Jackpot—the full-size M&M's bags given out by the Packers earlier being THE JACKPOT. After taking a millisecond to think it over, they unanimously agree with Phil on the timing and head for the Winnys' house.

As they approach the house next door to the Winnys', a speeding car races past, hastily turns onto their driveway, and rolls into the garage. As the automated garage door closes behind the car, the gang sees Mrs. Winny exiting the car and running into the house.

No other trick-or-treaters are nearby. Presumably because word has spread that no one is home. Everything seems to be setting up perfectly.

"Let's go!" exclaims Mike as the gang begins running toward the porch.

They arrive, with Mooch bringing up the rear, and take a moment to catch their breaths. They smile with eager anticipation as Mike reaches out to ring the doorbell. *Ding-dong.* Their heads spin with Reese's Pieces fantasies only a twelve-year-old boy can conjure—being drenched by a shower of, jumping into a deep pool full of, or floating down a raging river of the peanut butter–filled candies.

"Trick-or-treat!"

"Perfect timing, boys," says Mrs. Winny as she excitedly opens the door.

The boys look at each other with opportunistic smiles. They're about to pull off one of their greatest Halloween achievements.

After a long look at Mooch and then Cruz, perhaps recognizing them from the grocery store the other day, Mrs. Winny slowly reaches into a large deep bowl she has carried to the door.

"This is your lucky day. I think you'll be pleased with what we have for you this evening," she says, pulling out *two family-size bags* of Reese's Pieces and handing them to Mike and Phil. She then reaches back into the bowl for *two more* large bags of Reese's Pieces. She pauses for a second look at Mooch and Cruz, thinking to herself that they look familiar in some way before hesitantly handing over the candy. Mooch and Cruz carefully accept the candy, unsure if Mrs. Winny will follow through or change her mind and decide to withhold the prize.

With candy securely stowed in their bags, the gang shouts, "Thank you!"

"You're very welcome, boys. Enjoy!" she says as the gang turns and walks away, victorious.

It was a SPECTACULAR sight. The glossy bags of candy seemed to be glowing neon orange during the transaction—a true gift from the Candy Gods! Clearing the corner of the garage, now out of sight from the front porch, they pause to relish the supreme accomplishment with a triumphant scream and another round of mega high fives.

With their celebration complete, they make their way onto the sidewalk, where they spot the Rookie Gang across the street.

"So much for all that elaborate planning you guys love to brag about! Nobody's home over there! Ha!" yells Jimmy Krisyzniak, leader of the Rookie Gang, laughing.

"Yeah, well played!" adds Buck Thompson, Jimmy's sidekick, as he and their other cohorts, the Brooks twins, join in the laughter.

Angered by their astonishing combination of supreme arrogance and stupidity, Mooch quickly retorts, "You guys have no idea what you're talk—"

Covering Mooch's mouth so he doesn't divulge to these yahoos that they're actually wrong, Phil revises Mooches reply, "Yeah, you win some, and you lose some, I guess."

"Guess you guys aren't so smart after all, huh? Not so much the experts you claim to be!" prods Jimmy.

Mooch can't take any more lip from these punks. He spins out of Phil's grasp and yells, "Well, for your information—"

In escaping Phil's grasp, Mooch bumps into Cruz, who quickly grabs him and covers his mouth for a second time, allowing an opening for Mike to provide another revised reply, "Guess not."

Cruz slowly releases his grasp of Mooch as Phil turns to him and whispers through his clenched teeth, "Mooch. Cool it! You're going to give it up to these mega clowns that the Winnys are home and give them the chance to score big."

"Argh! Okay . . . But how dare *they* question *us*! How dare *they* call *us* out! They—" Mooch, stopped by a shove in the gut from Phil, crouches over in pain. "Ow! What the—?"

"Mooch! Stop it or you'll tip these morons off—their loss, our gain. It's about the candy, not the glory, remember? Let it go," whispers Mike sternly.

Now kneeling on the ground in pain, Mooch nods his head in acknowledgement. Mike helps him to his feet, pats him on the back, and gestures for him to stay calm.

"Next time, how about you just give me a nudge on the shoulder or a slap on the face instead of punching me in the stomach? Not cool on Halloween. Have to keep the stomach in perfect working order tonight—punching it doesn't help," Mooch says to Phil.

"Sorry, you just wouldn't stop. I couldn't let those dorks know what we got. They don't deserve it."

As they regroup to commence with the remainder of their journey, Pip and his friends approach.

"Everyone's saying nobody's home here. Did you guys go to this house?" asks Pip, wondering why Mike and his buddies would waste their time here if no one were home.

"You should give it a try," whispers Mike, smiling to his little brother.

Pip looks at him, confused. He then looks around in all directions and sees no one else in the vicinity except for Krisyzniak and his gang loitering across the street.

"Trust me," whispers Mike with his back to the Rookie Gang.

"Yeah, you'll be happy you did," adds Mooch under his breath.

Pip looks at Phil and Cruz and they deliver subtle nods of reassurance.

Still somewhat hesitant, Pip quietly replies, "Okay." He whispers to his friends, "Guys, let's give this house a shot."

They proceed cautiously up the driveway and disappear behind the corner of the garage. After about a minute they reemerge.

"Wow! Full bags of Reese's Pieces! WOOHOO!" they scream, holding their bags proudly high in the air.

Pip and his friends give Mike and the others huge high fives and then the two groups let out one more collective scream of exhilaration.

"Thanks for the tip, Mikey!" exclaims Pip.

"No problem, little bro," replies Mike, happy to help out his younger sibling.

In a trance of complete shock at what they just saw, the Rookie Gangs' jaws drop. Quickly snapping out of their daze, they run as fast as they can toward the Winnys' porch. As they reach the destination, they hear the front door lock and see the porch light go dark. Frantically they ring the doorbell—but it's no use, they've missed their window of opportunity. The garage door opens, and the Winnys' car backs out and speeds down the street.

"How about that planning, Krisyzniak?!" yells Mooch as he and the rest of the gang laugh.

The Rookie Gang can do nothing but hang their heads in defeat as they pass by. This is the much-deserved retribution for their earlier ignorant nastiness and, accordingly, Mike's Gang celebrates this moment of justice with another round of high fives as they scream "WOOHOO!"

"Okay, come on, guys. We still have a lot to do," Mike reminds them.

They refocus on the TOTR and move down the street with purpose.

25

The Clarks'

Energized from visiting the Hotters' house and exhilarated by the score at the Winnys', the gang is ready for phase two of the night—Cherry Grove, the wealthy neighborhood just north of theirs. Based on historical experience, it will surely have an abundance of houses with exceptional candy opportunities. Seeing Josh's Crew walking toward the main thoroughfare connecting the two neighborhoods, Orchard Street, the gang knows they're now headed to Cherry Grove as well. Focused on staying ahead of the merciless crew, the gang runs as fast as they can to the front gate of the Clarks' yard.

Mike and Cruz arrive first. Phil arrives second, more behind than usual because he had an incident along the way—his glasses broke again! This time it's not the frame, still strongly intact from his earlier ingenious repair, but the left lens. While running at full speed, his hand inadvertently hit the glasses, causing the lens to jar loose, fall, and bounce along the ground. Upon reaching the others, Phil stops abruptly and opens his hand to reveal the chipped and scratched lens. Panting to catch his breath from the run, he wastes no time chitchatting and goes straight into repair mode.

"What the—?! Again?!" asks Mike.

Phil shakes his head in disbelief and replies, "Yeah, can you believe it? Was hoping we had our last glitch for the night. Guess not."

Several seconds later, an out-of-breath Mooch finally arrives, stomping the pavement with a slow, heavy shuffle. Gasping for air, he stops and bends over, putting his hands on his knees for support. After taking

157

several more seconds to catch his breath, he raises his head to see Phil grunting as he tries to push the lens back into the frame of his glasses.

"Again?!" asks Mooch.

"It won't go in! I'm afraid if I push any harder, I might break the lens, or possibly the splint. Argh!" exclaims Phil, aggravated. "Guess I'm going pirate for the rest of the night, guys."

The others are worried. It will be difficult to navigate the remainder of the route with only one good eye. Perhaps impossible, given that the only quick way to Cherry Grove is to traverse through the Clarks' yard—an expedition with many lurking dangers and, thus, one not to be taken lightly.

The neighborhood kids believe the Clarks' house is haunted. The neighborhood adults won't speak about it much, revealing only that long ago the Clarks were very nice and happy people but then something went horribly wrong. Rumor has it the house is haunted by Mrs. Clark, the long-time resident who was allegedly murdered by her husband there six years earlier. Mr. Clark has never been seen since that horrible incident. People say he was most likely sent to prison, and the house has remained vacant with all the Clarks' belongings left untouched inside. Due to the prolonged vacancy, the house and yard have become run-down and in need of many repairs.

As a by-product of all the horrific stories surrounding the Clarks' house, the gang considers Clark Bars taboo (they're the "forbidden candy") for fear of inciting the sinister Clark Curse upon eating them. As such, Clark Bars are not to be consumed under any circumstance—a rule that has been strictly enforced and devoutly obeyed ever since they started trick-or-treating together. Well, obeyed by all except Mooch, who secretly enjoys Clark Bars on occasion, unable to resist their chocolaty goodness.

While placing the lens securely in one of the side pockets of his backpack, Phil summarizes the planned route one last time—the shortest path to the desired exit point, around the right side of the house and away from the dreaded shed in the far-left corner of the yard. The others nervously nod their heads in acknowledgement. Phil commences the expedition by inching slowly and cautiously forward. Not quite ready to advance, the other three remain still, afraid of the dangers that undoubtedly await.

"C'mon, guys! We have to move. Now!" exclaims Phil, noticing that he's the only one advancing.

"Okay, okay. But are you sure you can make it with only one eye?" asks Mike, concerned that Phil is perhaps taking too risky a chance.

"Yeah, feels pretty risky. Maybe we should bag this idea and just head down Orchard Street like always," suggests Mooch.

"If we do that, we lose way too much time and risk something much worse—getting to all those houses handing out amazing candy too late and potentially missing out! Plus, Josh and his goons have a head start on us if we go that way. This is the big league, guys. Cherry Grove!" pleads Phil.

"You sure you can make it? It's gonna be dangerous. Maybe Cruz and I go through the yard and you and Mooch go around? Any houses we hit before you get there, we'll just split the candy with you," offers Mike.

"Split? Did you say *split* the candy? I don't know about that," says Mooch. "That's not what we're about. That's not what this night is about—"

"Guys, we need Phil if we're going to do this. We either all go through or all go around," says Cruz.

After pausing for a second to think it over, Mike concedes, "Yeah, I guess."

"Look, I'm going through, plain and simple. This has always been and will always be the plan. I can do this. I can't—I won't—let you guys down. Trust me," demands Phil.

Mike gives Phil a long look. He can see Phil is serious and completely committed to the success of this mission. He looks at Mooch and Cruz, reading on their faces that they're in as well. "Okay, let's do this."

Cruz pumps his fist in excitement.

Mooch smiles but he's still hesitant. He's scared for his friend, and for himself. He also wonders if, for once, he won't be the one slowing the gang down. Then, as he often does when nervous, he reaches into his bag for a piece of candy to settle himself down. Preoccupied with the potential terrors that lie ahead, he mistakenly grabs a piece of Mrs. Baker's homemade "candy," slowly unwraps it, and places it in his mouth.

Just as the piece reaches Mooch's tongue, Phil notices the tragedy that is about to occur and screams out, "Wait! That's a piece of—"

Mooch closes his mouth.

"—Mrs. Baker's candy!" finishes Phil.

Instantly, a look of horror comes over Mooch's face in anticipation of experiencing an awful flavor.

Mike, Phil, and Cruz look upon him with shock, their mouths wide open in wonderment about what will happen next.

Mooch freezes, clenching his jaws tight, and stares into the distance in fear, as the piece of candy rests motionless in his mouth. After a few seconds, he begins slowly chewing the candy and proclaims, "Hmm . . . Surprisingly NOT bad, not bad at all. Actually, it's amazing!"

"Really?!" asks Phil.

"Huh, how about that?! Who would've thought?" says Mike as Cruz smiles and shakes his head in disbelief.

"Coconut-chocolate-banana. Delicious!"

Refocusing on the task at hand, Mike and Cruz begin carefully surveying the Clarks' front yard, house, and as much of the backyard as they can see. Mike wonders one last time if this is a good idea, but then decides they've come too far to turn back now—they must forge on. He gathers his cape and tucks it down the back of his shirt to avoid any potential for a snag. Turning around to give a final pep talk to Mooch and Phil, Mike sees the two of them putting on their vampire capes again.

"What're you guys doing?" asks Mike as Cruz stands looking at them with his arms spread out wide, palms up in the air.

"We're putting on our stealth gear. We want to be as invisible as possible—like ninja warriors. With these capes on we'll be nearly impossible to see in the dark—invisible!" replies Phil.

With a look of complete confusion, Mike asks, "Who's going to see us?"

"I don't know, the ghost of Mrs. Clark or any number of other scary creatures that may be lurking come to mind," retorts Mooch.

"Why didn't you guys just dress up as Dracula this year? You've worn those costumes as much as your real ones tonight," remarks Cruz as he removes his Terminator sunglasses and stashes them in his backpack. He and Mike share a chuckle.

"The cape clearly puts you guys in the unacceptable costumes category. Using it for isolated times like second visits is *temporary* and so, a semi-acceptable loophole. But you guys have gone way beyond that with this—especially now," states a frustrated Mike. "We're about to enter a dangerous situation and those capes could get caught on something and slow us down when we need to move fast. Wearing them *is not* a good idea, at all."

As Mooch and Phil look at each other and shrug, Phil replies, "We need every edge we can get. We'd rather take advantage of the 'stealthiness' the capes give us and take our chances with the 'safety' concerns."

With the argument completed and Phil and Mooch now transformed back into vampires, they all take a deep breath and commence entry into the dark and dreary yard through its dilapidated black-iron gate. After taking only a couple of steps, a black cat dashes in front of them, stops, and looks back at them inquisitively. With the moonlight reflecting mesmerizingly off its eyes, the boys' hearts all skip a beat as they freeze in fear. The cat takes a few unnerving moments to study the boys and then darts away toward the house and into the darkness. They collectively exhale as Mooch voices serious second thoughts about the entire undertaking.

"Uh, guys . . . I think maybe we should *definitely* turn around now and head down Orchard Street."

Getting angry with Mooch's lack of commitment and courage, Cruz replies, "No! Let's go—move!"

Mike calms Cruz with a hand gesture and motions to Mooch to follow him into the yard. "You want to get revenge on Josh and his crew for last year or not?"

Mooch nods his head affirmatively, takes another deep breath, and cautiously follows Mike.

Meanwhile, Phil has been meticulously surveying the yard through a pair of mini-binoculars (using only his one good eye) and has devised a small, simplifying revision to the route. They had intended to go over the six-foot-high solid wood fencing separating the front yard from the backyard on the *right* side of the house because it's closer to where they believe the best exit point is in the backyard. They've only been able to study a small portion of the property, so this theory is based more on a hunch than on recon. Most of the Clarks' yard is blocked from view by numerous overgrown trees and bushes. However, during his impromptu survey, Phil notices what he thinks is a hole in the fence leading to the backyard on the *left* side of the house. Presumably this existing hole will allow an easier entry.

"Guys, we should go on the left side of the house. I think I see a hole we can get though."

Mooch is rattled by this sudden change and, being superstitious, recommends they stick to the original plan. He reminds them that going *right* (which is another way of saying *correct*) is safer than going left (which, as the opposite of right, is *wrong*). Seeing the hole for themselves, Mike and Cruz have no choice but to agree with Phil—much to Mooch's dismay.

Hesitantly, the foursome tiptoes ever so quietly up to and around the left corner of the house, their shirts and capes scraping ominously along the peeling paint protruding from the house's white siding. As they move closer to the fence, suddenly a creaking sound comes from inside the house! They instantly stop, eyes WIDE in horror. After a few moments of listening ever so intently for, but not hearing, another noise, they proceed.

"Guys, we should use the flashlights," whispers Mooch.

"We can't. The light would give up our position. We'd be sitting ducks," whispers Phil.

Letting out a moan of frustration and fear, Mooch glances over his shoulder to the front gate and contemplates making a run for it. Figuring that route would be equally scary at this point, he scurries forward to be close to the others.

Mike is first to reach the fence. He carefully crouches and pokes his head through the hole. He looks left, then right, then down, then up, and then left again. Seeing no sign of danger, he crawls through the hole, reaching the other side safely. Phil is next, assisted by Mike. Third is Mooch, pulled by Mike from the front and pushed by Cruz from behind. He needs help from both ends squeezing through an opening barely big enough for his large frame. Halfway through he catches his vampire cape on the edge of the hole, abruptly stopping his forward momentum. Panicked, he begins violently tugging on the cape in an effort to free it from the fence. After a couple stronger tugs, the cape tears, causing him to lunge forward. Losing his balance, he falls awkwardly to the side, ripping his right pant leg and scratching his knee—his streak of dirtying his costume still intact. Now bleeding, Mooch screams in pain—Mike immediately covers his mouth to muffle him.

"I told you the capes were a *bad* idea," whispers Mike. Waiting a couple seconds for Mooch to calm down, Mike slowly removes his hand from his mouth and then helps him to his feet, allowing the opening required for Cruz to quickly slip through the hole.

With the first segment of the expedition now complete, however unorthodox it may have been, the gang continues the journey through the backyard. In addition to having all the stories about Mrs. Clark's horrific death and how her ghost haunting the house in the forefront of their minds, they've been told about other fearsome obstacles in the Clarks' yard. Legend has it that the ghost of the Clarks' Doberman pinscher still guards the property, deterring any and all trespassers who dare to enter. With this legend prominently in their thoughts, they pass the back corner of the house.

CREAK! blares another noise, this time louder and more definitive. Mike and Cruz, who are closest to the house, identify that it's coming from inside the unlit back corner room, presumably the kitchen. Mooch and Phil, however, hear the sound coming from the shed up ahead in the back corner of the yard. Mooch freezes in fear as the other three continue forward. Noticing that Mooch isn't moving, Mike emphatically waves at him to get going.

"Mooch! C'mon!" he whispers.

Phil adds quietly, "Yeah—"

"WOO!" screams a group of kids in the distance, cutting off Phil and jolting Mooch into jumping forward.

Now all moving together again, they pass by the rear corner of the house. Phil sees what looks like a dog to the right of the shed. He nudges Mike, who quickly turns to look toward the same image. *Is this the ghost of the Clarks' Doberman pinscher?!* Mike then quietly pokes at Mooch and Cruz as he points out the figure in the distance.

Already consumed by fearful thoughts of ghosts racing through his head, Mooch begins to scream and is again instantly quieted by a hand covering his mouth—this time Cruz's. The foursome stops and scrunches close to the ground, watching terrified as the form slowly moves toward them, looking more and more like a dog—*like a ghost dog!* Their hearts racing, they begin to wonder if they should turn and run—if they do, they can still get out alive!

Just as Mooch reaches his limit and begins to rise in preparation for running, the image comes into a sliver of moonlight. It's the black cat they saw earlier, but now it has a small leafy branch stuck to its back that forms the shape of dog-like ears! Letting out a collective loud sigh of relief, they spook the cat, causing it to jump in the air. As it flees behind the shed, the leafy branch dislodges from its back and falls to the ground.

Now safely past the "ghost dog," they continue toward the back fence. Passing by the corner of the shed, the gang peers through the open door into the dark space inside—nothing can be seen moving in there—a good sign. They now turn toward the back fence of the yard, only about fifteen yards away. Beginning to think they're in the clear with no noticeable danger ahead, the wind suddenly picks up out of nowhere and rain begins to lightly fall. This immediately throws them back into panic mode as another creaking noise is heard—this time it's definitely coming from the shed.

Mooch mumbles, "Rain! It never rains on Halloween. This is a very bad omen." He decides he can't take any more of this. As he takes the first step of his quick retreat, Mooch steps directly on his cape. With the grass now slick from the rain, the cape slides along the ground, causing him to fall onto his back. The momentum of the fall combined with the slick ground facilitates a continued slide forward and eventually down into a large hole!

He lands at the bottom of the hole and screams for help as the others immediately turn their heads looking for Mooch—*where has he gone?!*

"Mooch?!" screams out Mike.

"Over here!" replies Mooch, shrieking from the hole.

Hearing Mooch's voice, Mike runs to the hole, slides on his belly to the edge, and looks down. Mooch is about eight feet down in what looks like an old degraded well! Thankfully it's been filled with random debris over the years and isn't too deep. Mike extends his arm in an attempt to reach Mooch, but can't connect with his outstretched arm below. With the wind and rain intensifying, the gang is becoming increasingly panicked.

Mooch tries to climb up the sheer vertical sides of the hole, but it's too slippery from the rain. Phil reaches for his costume's whip to pull Mooch from the hole and discovers it's missing—it must have fallen off earlier in the journey. As an alternate plan, Phil proposes Mooch take off his cape and throw one end of it up to him to use as a makeshift rope with which, the others can pull him to safety. He adds that he will throw one end of his cape down to Mooch so they can twist the two into one rope to provide double the strength.

Mooch thinks he sees and hears creatures coming through the sides of the hole and, thus, wants out immediately! In panic mode, he complies with Phil's request, removing his cape as quickly as possible and launching one end upward. Simultaneously, Phil lowers one end of his down to Mooch. As Mike catches the end of Mooch's, he wonders internally if even this double strength cape-rope will be able to withstand Mooch's weight, but figures they have no other options and no time to waste. As Mooch joins the ends of the two capes together, Mike does the same and gives the capes a few quick twists. Phil and Cruz then grab hold and the trio commence pulling. With all their collective might, and Mooch scurrying with vigor up the side of the hole, they eventually raise him to safety.

All four now lying on the ground and breathing heavily from the struggle, Mooch asks if his trick-or-treat bag is okay. The integrity of his candy is always his primary concern.

Phil rolls to his side to see it resting on the ground next to Mooch. "Yes. It's still with us. Good thing my dad waterproofed it."

"That was a close one. Thank god we had the capes for you guys to pull me up."

"Your cape is *the reason* you fell down the hole in the first place!" retorts Cruz.

Mike again has to calm Cruz. Then he refocuses the others on completing the mission. With the wind and rain subsiding, they all rise and gather their things. Phil and Mooch start to move forward, but Mike stops them.

"Okay, capes off. Now! In the hole!" demands Mike, gesturing that they must leave them behind, with Cruz standing next to him, arms crossed, nodding in agreement.

Reluctantly but understandably, Phil and Mooch comply by ceremoniously dropping them into the dark pit. They all move toward the back fence, careful to avoid the pit.

Well, three of them anyway. With the one lens of his glasses now covered in raindrops and splashes of mud, Phil can hardly see. He walks slowly, arms outstretched in a feeble attempt to "feel" his way forward. This technique fails catastrophically as his right foot slips on the edge of the pit. In an instant Phil realizes he'll soon be at the bottom of the pit facing the very same challenge his friend just overcame.

"Ah!" he screams in desperation, his foot sliding down.

"Gotcha!" yells Mike, grabbing him by the arm and dragging him to safety.

"Whew! Thanks! That was close!" replies a relieved Phil.

"Too close," adds Mooch. "Way to go, Mikey!"

"I'll help you the rest of the way out of here, buddy," comforts Mike.

Having avoided what they all very much hope will be the last challenge of the night, and desperately ready to exit this horrifying yard, they arrive at the back fence.

"Okay, we're going to have to jump over. I'll go over first, then Phil, then Mooch, and Cruz last," outlines Mike.

Mike hops up, grabs the top of the fence with both hands, and deftly pulls himself up and over.

Landing safely on the other side, he calls, "Okay, Phil. You're next."

Cruz interlocks his hands to create a foothold for Phil. Phil quickly steps on Cruz's hands, grabs his shoulder, and hoists himself up to grab the top of the fence. He then awkwardly pulls himself over while Mike helps him to the ground on the other side.

"Okay, now you, Mooch. Let's go," says Mike.

Cruz again offers his interlocked hands and Mooch places his foot in them. As he grabs Cruz's shoulder and begins to hoist himself upward—another loud creaking noise comes from the house. Mooch and Cruz look at each other in absolute fear; Mike and Phil do the same on the other side of the fence. Mooch and Cruz then slowly turn to look toward the left back corner of the house to see a large shadow coming toward them.

"AHH! It's the ghost of Mrs. Clark!" yells Mooch.

"AHH!" yells Cruz.

"Hurry!" yell Mike and Phil.

Did the shadow come from the house or the shed?! As the shadow moves slowly closer it looks like a large figure with something sticking up from its head—*is it a horn?!*

In complete terror, Cruz attempts to thrust Mooch upward and over the fence, but slips (the bottom of his shoes are slippery from the rain) and falls forward into the fence, losing control of Mooch. Mooch falls on top of Cruz.

The shadow is nearly upon them—*is this the end?!* As they begin to cover their faces in fear, a hand reaches and grabs Mooch's arm. It's Mike! He has extended his arm through a hole in the fence created by the fall they just had! Mooch scurries through as Mike drags him out and Cruz pushes him forward. As he rolls through the hole to safety, Cruz feels the hand of the shadow brush against his foot.

Terrified, they all jump to their feet and run across the street, away from the fence to safety. Breathing heavily, exhausted from the gauntlet they've just survived, the gang stares at the hole in the fence.

"That was a close one," says Mike.

"I don't think we should *ever* try that again. EVER!" exclaims Phil.

"I second that. Happy HORRORween," replies Mooch as Mike and Cruz shake their heads in agreement.

Always prepared, Phil takes a bandage from his backpack and gives it to Mooch for the cut on his knee. Mooch nods his thanks to Phil. After Mooch is done placing the bandage, they gather their things and walk away from this experience feeling they've achieved a *major accomplishment*, while simultaneously dodging a *major bullet*.

26

Josh's Crew

Earlier in the week, Josh and his goons had heard from Terry McDowell (just like last year) that Mike's Gang was planning to stash candy at a location along their trick-or-treating route (just like last year). This news has Josh mega excited. It's consuming his every thought and every move.

According to Terry's intel, by this time in the evening, Mike and his gang should have hidden their stash in Collins Park. Collins Park is their neighborhood playground, on the northeast corner of Fossil Way and Orchard Street—an ideal location that's on the way to and from Cherry Grove. Eager to take advantage of this supreme opportunity to once again pilfer the gang's loot, Josh and his extended crew (including Lisa, Roni, and Terry) hurry as fast as they can to the park.

They arrive to find the park devoid of people—eerily quiet, blanketed with an ominous and spooky aura, and dimly lit in the cloud-covered moonlight. While waiting for a couple other groups of kids to pass by down Orchard Street, Bobby carefully surveys the park to verify that Mike and his gang are nowhere to be found. The coast is clear, a positive indicator that they must have already been here to stash their loot!

"Okay, guys, spread out and find that stash!" commands Josh excitedly as all four boys pull flashlights from their bags.

Not all members of the crew are as excited and focused on stealing the gang's stash as Josh. Travis Bennett, for one. "We're wasting too much time. We might miss out on the good stuff in Cherry Grove if this takes too long."

Since he's the lowest-ranking member of the crew and therefore *never* listened to, the others disregard his concern. They don't even pause to give him a look.

Rob isn't entirely fond of Josh's plan either. He feels guilty about repeating the offense of stealing their candy, particularly when they already had their fun with this sort of thing last year. Why pile on? But, as is his way, Rob keeps his feelings to himself. He doesn't want to experience the wrath from Josh that would inevitably ensue.

"I can't wait to find their loot!" Bobby proclaims. "I'm going to wave it around in front of Mooch's fat face the second I see him! He's gonna be so mad—it's gonna be great!"

"Yeah, I'm gonna eat a bunch of Mike's pieces right in front of him and watch him drool and then cry like a baby!" adds Josh. "And what's up with you? You don't seem very excited either," he continues, now turning his attention to Rob.

"No . . . I am," answers Rob, in as convincing a voice as he can muster.

Lisa is with Travis on this one, which is highly unusual. No one can recall an instance when Lisa and Travis agreed on anything. To clarify, Lisa agrees with Travis as it pertains to the *what* (that they shouldn't be attempting to steal the gang's stash), but not so much as it pertains to the *why* (that it will waste time). She believes stealing is WRONG, period. And particularly from a friend like Mike. She couldn't care less about the time it may take away from trick-or-treating.

"Guys, this is wrong! You should *not* be stealing their candy. They worked hard to get it—it's *theirs* to keep!" exclaims Lisa.

"Yeah, it's not right stealing other people's stuff. You guys are awful," agrees Roni.

Having stated their cases strongly, Lisa and Roni look to Terry, expecting her to agree with them. Conflicted by her allegiance to her friends versus her desire to please Josh, she elects to remain silent and just shrugs her shoulders.

"Well, we haven't stolen it yet, and we're not going to if we keep wasting time with this nonsense. Look, being girls, you just don't understand these sorts of things. We have to take advantage of this—this is way too juicy an opportunity to pass up!" replies Bobby.

"Yeah, we've been waiting for this all year. We're not going to stop now. This is what Halloween is all about—grabbing as much candy as you can get, any way you can," adds Josh.

Completely disregarding the girls' opinions, Josh and Bobby hastily begin their search. After a few steps, they notice that the girls, as well as Travis and Rob, aren't following. They stop and look back angrily.

"You *girls* not coming?" asks Josh, implying that all five of them are "girls."

Travis remains motionless, waiting for someone else to make the first move. Rob is speechless—torn between doing what he knows is right and risking the wrath of Josh versus just going with the flow and avoiding confrontation. Terry is stuck awkwardly in the middle—torn between staying loyal to her friends versus her longing to be with Josh. She stands next to Lisa and Roni, unsure of what to do.

"No way. You can definitely count us out," responds Lisa, as Roni shakes her head to display her refusal as well.

"Okay, suit yourselves," replies Josh. Then he sees Rob isn't moving forward. "You too?!" asks Josh.

"Yeah, this just isn't right. I can't be a part of this anymore," replies Rob.

Josh glares back at Rob and shakes his head in disappointment. "What?! What's with you tonight? Come on, enough of this—let's go!"

But for the first time ever, Rob doesn't budge, deciding definitively that he's not going. He's been pushed to his limit; he's done with Josh's shenanigans.

Somewhat impressed by Rob's unprecedented act of courage, Josh gives a subtle nod of acceptance before disappointedly heading off with Bobby closely by his side.

Unable to build up the courage to risk a confrontation with Josh, Travis gives the girls and Rob a quick glance and scurries off behind Josh.

Lisa and Roni turn away in disgust and angrily head off in the opposite direction toward Orchard Street, hoping to cross paths with Mike and his gang in Cherry Grove.

Internally heartbroken that Josh didn't specifically ask her along—directing his attention to everyone but her—Terry remains still, staring at Josh as he fades into the darkness. She slowly turns and follows dejectedly behind the girls.

As Rob heads off in a different direction from all the others, he calls back to the girls, "Tell those guys I'm sorry for the bad stuff we've done. Tell them I'm done with hanging around Josh."

After searching for what seems like forever, Travis is becoming increasingly concerned that the hunt is taking too long. Again, he suggests they call it off and continue to Cherry Grove. The others ignore him and continue searching intently—their desire to find the stash increasing with every passing moment. After several more minutes, Bobby stumbles on something promising. It's a cooler! Stashed behind a rock and under a bush in the farthest corner of the park!

"JACKPOT!" he yells.

The others stop in their tracks and run toward Bobby to feast their eyes on the presumed prize. The cooler is a glorious site, brightly "glowing" in the moonlight like a sparkling treasure chest. Their mouths water from the thought of all the delicious candy inside and the excitement of pulling off yet another coup against their arch-rivals. Their anticipation is all-consuming. Josh kneels next to the cooler and slowly opens the top to reveal the contents. NOTHING! Nothing except an assortment of suckers in various flavors and a handwritten note: "SURPRISE, SUCKERS! NO CANDY FOR YOU TO STEAL THIS YEAR!"

Josh yells out at the top of his lungs as he jumps to his feet and ushers his friends to move forward out of the park, "Let's go! Cherry Grove, guys. NOW!"

They begin running and in short order approach the exit from the park. As they pass through the gate, Travis notices an object under a nearby bush and sidetracks to inspect it.

"Hey, guys, check this out!" he shouts before kneeling down to examine another cooler.

Hoping the first cooler was merely a diversionary tactic and the real stash is still here, the others kneel next to Travis as he swiftly opens this second one. NOTHING! Again! Nothing but another handwritten note: "NOTHING HERE EITHER! SEE YOU ON THE OTHER SIDE, SUCKERS!" And a pile of empty sucker wrappers that look suspiciously like the ones they left in the gang's stash container last year.

Now as angry as he's ever been (and that's saying something), Josh leaps to his feet and runs off, his fists tightly clenched, in the direction of Cherry Grove. Bobby and Travis scurry in his wake.

Hardly able to contain his anger at wasting time on *two* wild-goose chases, Josh is determined to get to Cherry Grove as quickly as possible, find the gang, and seek revenge. *HOW DARE THEY embarrass ME! They will pay for this!*

Up ahead, almost to Cherry Grove, Lisa begins to wonder how Josh knew Mike's Gang would be storing their candy in the park. Thinking it through as she walks, methodically eliminating all the sources it couldn't be, she eventually narrows it down to the only one it could be—Terry. *It had to be Terry. She's always trying to extract information from Mooch, and she's always desperate to feed information to Josh.* "Weird the way those guys knew Mike and his gang would be hiding their candy in the park this year," she says.

"Yeah, I was just wondering the same thing. How could they have known that? Mike and his gang keep that kind of stuff very secret," Roni observes.

"Someone must have spilled it. It had to be someone who regularly interacts with both Mike's and Josh's groups. Someone who's good at getting information from one side and feeding it to the other," Lisa continues.

Sensing that Lisa is on to her, Terry continues staring at the ground, desperately racking her brain for an excuse, an alibi, or a scapegoat. After a few seconds, she can think of nothing, and defeat begins to creep over her. She's surely busted.

Pressing the topic, now looking directly at Terry, Lisa continues, "It must have been someone who—"

"All right! All right. It was me. Getting the goods from Mooch was like taking candy from a baby. It was *so* easy. *Too* easy! And it was such *juicy* information, I couldn't resist—I just *had* to tell Josh," Terry blurts. "Plus, you wanted revenge on Mike for backing out on you!"

Upon hearing this, Roni stares at Terry with her mouth open wide. Allowing a few seconds to let what she's just heard fully sink in, Roni's expression progressively turns from shock to disappointment. She recalls that this sort of thing has happened several times before.

Lisa isn't shocked. She'd already pieced it together in her mind and she isn't happy with Terry, at all. It's true that Lisa was mad at Mike, but what Terry did was wrong, more wrong than what Josh and his friends are currently doing. Terry aided and abetted a theft—to make matters worse, theft from her beloved Mike and his gang. Lisa shakes her head at Terry to show that this was a step too far.

As they move forward together in silence—Lisa angry, Roni disappointed, and Terry embarrassed—they each continue to individually contemplate the situation. Lisa suppresses her anger toward Terry and resolves to spend the remainder of the night helping Mike and his friends get their candy back and, if possible, now taking revenge on Josh. Roni can see that Lisa is now laser-focused on helping Mike and, as always, will stand by to assist her friend in accomplishing this task.

Terry slowly acknowledges that what she did was wrong, and she begins to feel bad for betraying Mooch so many times. Mooch would do anything for her, and she's ashamed she took advantage of him. The sadness she felt from Josh ignoring her earlier is shifting to anger. She's tired of Josh using her for information and giving her nothing in return. She decides she's going to help Mooch and his buddies however she can. It's payback time for Josh.

27

All That and More

The gang is feeling great! They made it to Cherry Grove in record time. All their hard work and planning paid off. Although it didn't go exactly as scripted, they still managed to get through the dreaded Clarks' yard mostly unharmed, save a few scary incidents and a small cut or bruise here and there. Seeing no sign of Josh and his crew, they assume the distractions they created at the park must have worked as they'd hoped.

"Pretty darn masterful how we managed to lure Josh and his goons on that wild-goose chase—had to cost them at least a half an hour. Mooch, I wasn't sure you were going to pull it off, but you did! Good job, buddy!" exclaims Phil.

"Yeah, nice one," Mike agrees. "You finally got the upper hand on Terry McDowell—you swindled the swindler! And Phil, what a great idea! One of your best ever!"

Phil and Mike are referring to the events that took place earlier in the week. As Terry was orchestrating her typical information-extraction maneuvers on Mooch while they entered the lunchroom together, he "accidentally" divulged this year's candy-stash location. The catch being that the location was a fake, a setup, to trick Josh and his crew using their mole, Terry. It was a perfectly executed, ingenious plan that paired seamlessly with Terry's constant eagerness to please Josh. But more satisfyingly, it quenched the gang's desire to enact some revenge on Josh's Crew for last year. It worked beautifully—the plan of all plans!

"Well, boys, I have to thank Josh and his goons for stimulating my anger. Last year's tragedy gave me the motivation to stay focused. I also have to thank Terry for staying true to who she is. I wasn't sure my 'acting' was going to be good enough to fool her. But her uncontrollable desire to get info from me and give it to Josh got the best of her," proclaims Mooch.

"Yeah, she never saw it coming!" replies Phil.

"She's not going to be happy when she finds out, and Josh will be *fuming*," adds Cruz.

Realizing Cruz is right, a wave of fear rolls over Mooch and Phil. They're beginning to comprehend that Josh will undoubtedly attempt retaliation. That's who he is.

"Well, it was just all in good fun," says Phil, trying to downplay what they did and convince himself it won't be a big deal to Josh.

"Unfortunately, I'm not so sure it's the kind of 'fun' Josh likes," replies Mike.

"Well, he deserves it! That thug does mean things to all sorts of kids, all the time," retorts Mooch, comforting himself by rationalizing their actions.

"They weren't harmed, just fooled. It shouldn't be a big deal," continues Phil.

"He does deserve it. What we did was a win for all the kids in the neighborhood, all the kids at school. He's done so many nasty things to us and so many others; it's time he got some payback. And we gave it to him. I don't regret it one bit," states Mike, noticing Phil and Mooch are becoming increasingly agitated. "We just need to stick together and look out for each other for a while, and we'll be fine."

"Yep," agrees Cruz as he gives Mooch and Phil a look of reassurance.

"How about you, buddy?! Getting though the Clarks' with just one eye!" says Mike, shifting the conversation to a more positive topic.

"Yeah! That was awesome!" adds Mooch. "You were like that blind superhero . . . um . . . ah . . . Daredevil!"

"Ha! Yeah, I wasn't sure it was going to turn out too well—especially halfway through the yard—but I made it!" replies Phil.

As they move through the Cherry Grove neighborhood, all their candy dreams are coming true. Another house is giving out full-size chocolate bars—Twix! Other houses are handing out large Laffy Taffy and AirHeads, big boxes of Nerds, long Starburst packets, and much more. Score! So much great candy that their bags and backpacks become *packed* like never before!

The candy is fantastic, but the true highlight of Cherry Grove is, as always, the Hantes' house. Every year, the Hantes completely transform their driveway, front yard, and garage into an indoor-outdoor haunted house that kids from Cherry Grove and the surrounding neighborhoods all flock to.

By the time the gang arrives, the haunted house is jam-packed! Way more than even the Hotters' house! Mr. Hante is dressed up as his usual Frankenstein and Mrs. Hante as her typical Elvira, Mistress of the Dark! Her beauty isn't quite to the standard set by Mrs. Hotter, but she's a close second, looking pretty amazing in her own right.

Navigating through the haunted house takes a good ten minutes—ten minutes with all senses continuously peaked. The layout is a winding path with a variety of scary scenes that incorporate startling elements around every corner. Strobe lights strategically create a sense of disorientation that allows Mr. Hante to sneak in and out of scenes, spooking all who partake. In order of how they're experienced, the scenes are: a cornfield with the scariest scarecrow imaginable; Frankenstein's laboratory, complete with a realistic lightning bolt to generate power; Dracula's lair with Dracula sporadically leaping out of his coffin toward the trick-or-treaters at unsuspecting moments; a werewolf's den that features a full moon in the distant sky and ominous sounds of the creature lurking in the surrounding darkness; a chaotic and unnerving scene full of the "evil" creatures from the movie *Gremlins*; and the grand finale, the living room from *Poltergeist* with a young girl sitting in front of a TV, mesmerized by the pure static playing on the screen and listening to the associated crackling sound blaring from the speaker. Using the very best technology available to create an intense and exhilarating experience, each and every scene is both scary and fun!

After successfully negotiating the haunted house, the gang finds Mr. Poppy (the next-door neighbor) dressed up as the one and only Willy Wonka passing out Pop Rocks packets—three each, your choice of flavor! Watermelon is Mike's choice, grape for Mooch, strawberry for Phil, and cherry for Cruz (each purposely chooses the same flavor for all three packets). It just doesn't get any better than this. It's Halloween paradise.

"Happy HAUNTED-HOUSE-A-ween! How awesome was that?!" exclaims Mooch. "They *never* disappoint!"

"Best year ever! Super scary! Even in monovision," agrees Phil, referring to his current eyeglasses problem. "Got to hand it to the Hantes, they really know how to scare the HECK out of you. That was amazing!"

"How about the *Poltergeist* room—MEGA scary! Couldn't tell if she was real girl or a doll!" adds Mike.

"Oh, she was real—so scary!" replies Mooch.

"Nah, it was a doll. No real girl could sit that still for that long," says Phil.

"Yeah, maybe. Either way, it was scary. So, you guys want to try—"

"Don't even go there," orders Mike, cutting off Mooch midsentence. "We *are not* testing the soda-and-Pop Rocks combination death theory. We never do. You always stir this up, but none of us ever has the guts to try. Don't start."

"I'm not trying that. No way. Not a chance," states Phil while Cruz shakes his head, signaling he's out as well.

"Got it, Mikey?" asks Mike of Mooch, alluding to the Life cereal commercial featuring "Mikey," who was rumored (falsely) to have attempted the combination, tragically ending in his death.

Mooch takes a second or two to think and then decides against it, nodding his head in affirmation.

Having settled that issue (again), in unison they ceremoniously tear off the tops of the Pop Rocks packets, toast each other, and swiftly pour the entire contents of all three packets into their mouths. Thoroughly enjoying every second of the fizzy explosions, they talk to each other in garbled voices and tilt their heads to the side in an attempt to slow down the rate at which the rocks pop.

Having accomplished all missions planned for the night, they shake each other's hands, give each other a huge round of high fives, and begin the trek back to their neighborhood. As they walk, they relive the best, worst, and scariest moments of the evening and revel in how amazing the adventure was. They couldn't be happier. It was a great night! One for the ages!

"Well, it *was* a perfect night," says Mooch as he points down the street.

Up ahead in the distance he's spotted Josh and his pack of goons heading toward them and they *do not* look happy. But now Rob is missing and in his place is Josh's older brother, Brock. Brock is much bigger and meaner than Josh and loves any opportunity to pick on younger kids. *But why is he out trick-or-treating tonight? Isn't he too old for this sort of thing?*

Hoping Josh and his amended crew haven't seen them, the gang quickly and quietly scurries to the other side of the street. Reaching the destination successfully unnoticed (they think) and adeptly blending into the trick-or-treating herd (they hope), they feel relatively well camouflaged. However, Josh's Crew is quickly approaching and, by the look of things, diligently searching for them. They're aggressively swimming through the crowd, carefully examining everyone and everything they pass.

The gang realizes they have only two options—either move toward them stealthily through the crowd, hopefully slipping past unnoticed, or turn around and move in the other direction down the street, avoiding Josh's Crew altogether if they're lucky. Moving forward means returning home via Orchard Street—the safe and preferred route (assuming they avoid Josh). Turning around means going back through the Clarks' yard—the very unsafe and very *un*preferred route. No one wants to go through the Clarks' yard again, *no one!* But attempting to slip past Josh's Crew will be difficult and comes with mega-undesired consequences if they're caught.

With Josh surveying every inch of the street as he makes his way methodically toward them, and the amount of kids, and cover provided, between the gang and Josh diminishing with every step, the gang acknowledges their only real option. They must turn around and navigate the Clarks' yard yet again—but this time with no plan, bags completely full of candy, and Phil still with only one good eye.

28

The Clarks', Again

Maneuvering deftly through the groups of remaining trick-or-treaters, the gang quickly reaches the Clarks' back fence. Standing in front of the exit hole they used earlier in the evening, they stop to argue about whether or not this is the most prudent course of action.

"Maybe we should've just tried sneaking by them—we probably could've made it. Or if we had our vampire capes, we could've changed back into ninja mode and slid right on by them," Mooch suggests.

"But we *don't* have the vampire capes—and besides, we only had *two* of them anyway, not *four* like we need. We agreed it was gonna be too risky trying to pass them in the crowd. We agreed this way is the safer way," replies Mike.

"Yeah, but now thinking it through, we may have been able to hide in the crowd and let them just slide by," argues Phil with the fear of reentering the Clarks' yard swaying his judgment.

"You saw how angry Josh was—and his *big brother* is with him now! You saw him examining every square inch. No way we could've hidden— he would've found us for sure. Look, I know it's scary going back through this yard, but we can do it if we stick together," proclaims Mike, attempting to rally them ahead of the harrowing expedition.

"Hey there!" yells a voice from behind.

The boys pivot around in fearful anticipation. They're pleasantly surprised to see Lisa with Roni and Terry in tow approaching them slowly.

"How's it going, boys?" asks Lisa with her eyes fixed on Mike.

Relieved to see them, but anxious knowing he and his friends must quickly commence their getaway, Mike is short in his reply, "Uh, good. You?"

"We're good. What are you guys up to? Why are you way down here?" asks Lisa, wondering why they're standing outside the back fence of the most notorious house in their neighborhood.

"Uh, just heading back home. Got all the candy we can carry," replies Mike distractedly. The other three look around nervously, their heads swiveling back and forth as they watch for Josh and his crew.

"Okay. Well, we're going to head down Orchard Street now. Want to come with us?" asks Lisa.

"Did you get lots of good candy this year, Smoochy?" asks Terry, this time not in her typical condescending voice, but rather in a caring one. She feels bad for betraying him earlier (and doesn't yet know that Mooch actually set her up).

"Yes. A lot. I can hardly carry it all," replies Mooch. Terry's kindness takes him by surprise. He stops his surveillance of the area to proudly display the contents of his bag. "Good thing Phil created expandable backpacks—we couldn't have carried all our loot otherwise."

"You split up from Josh?" Mike asks Lisa.

"Yeah, we did. I'm not a fan of him, nor of his methods," she replies with a smile.

Mike can't help but smile big back at her, happy to hear this news.

Cruz hands Roni a Starburst, her favorite candy. She accepts it, blushing a little, and looks happily back at Cruz.

Mooch continues to show Terry his candy loot as she looks on with a new interest in and happiness for Mooch.

Phil remains preoccupied, conducting surveillance for Josh and his crew with his one good eye.

Meanwhile, Josh's anger isn't subsiding. It's growing. He's steaming mad and completely focused on his mission to confront the gang and take *all* their candy. He can't stand that they got the better of him. He'll show them who's king of the neighborhood once and for all. He's so completely determined to find them that he bypasses the coveted Hante house and works his way through the crowd—spinning around, shoving to the side, or knocking to the ground each kid he passes.

Not completely sharing in his exaggerated level of anger, and disappointed they're missing out on the grand prize of enjoying all Cherry Grove has to offer—*the best* candy and *the best* haunted house—Bobby and Travis follow behind Josh with his brother by his side.

"There they are!" yells Bobby, pointing up ahead about a hundred yards in the distance, excited he's found them and hoping the revenge will come swiftly so they can return to the Hantes' house before it's too late.

"Let's get 'em, boys," snarls Josh with a laser-beam stare as he begins to run forward.

While efficiently weaving his way through the crowd, Josh sees the gang talking with Lisa and her friends. They appear to be having a great time—joking, laughing, and sharing their stories and candy. Even Terry and Mooch appear to be genuinely getting along. This scene makes him even angrier—*Mike stole Lisa back?!* That makes it twice tonight that Mike has gotten the better of him—ARGH! As they seemingly say their good-byes, Lisa gives Mike a hug and then vanishes into the night with her friends.

Having not taken his eyes off the crew for a second, Phil alerts the others: "They spotted us! Here they come!"

The gang looks through what will be their reentry point into the yard, the hole in the fence that was created by Mooch's fall the first time they escaped. They look back to see Josh closing in on them and turn to each other one last time with fear in their eyes; they can't believe they have to do this AGAIN.

While Cruz wonders if the shadow will reemerge, Phil worries about his ability to see, and Mooch fears he won't be able to run fast enough, Mike leads the way, bravely squeezing through the hole first. Mooch is next and then Phil. Taking one last look back before he enters the hole, Cruz sees Josh's Crew nearly upon him and quickly ducks his head and slides through the hole.

"They're almost to the fence, guys," he whispers.

The clouds have increased, blocking most of the moonlight. It's much darker than it was earlier. Mike takes out his flashlight and turns it on. The light from the flashlight is dim—the batteries must be old! Having to move quickly, he has no choice but to carry on—this level of light will have to do.

Phil starts to remind Mike that using flashlights is too risky, but then quickly realizes at this point they need every advantage they can get. It's worth the risk of being seen.

Mike's first concern is finding and avoiding the pit that nearly swallowed Mooch, and then Phil. He thinks he knows where it is, but can't be entirely sure. Everything happened so fast the last time. He moves deliberately, sweeping his flashlight back and forth, the light scarcely illuminating the ground in front of him. He grows increasingly anxious when he thinks he hears Josh and his crew working their way through the hole in the fence, so he moves a little quicker with each step.

He feels a crunch under his foot and immediately looks down to see a piece of candy—Mrs. Baker's homemade candy. *This must be a piece that fell from one of our packs earlier.* Mike decides to look for another. Up ahead about five feet he finds another, and then another about ten feet ahead of that, and then another, and another, and so on until he reaches the hole in the fence leading to the front yard. Mike turns off his flashlight to make it harder for Josh's Crew to locate them. He quickly and quietly passes through the hole. The others follow close behind, one by one. Cruz is last, and he takes one last look back. He is surprised to see no sign of Josh or his goons.

Nearly in the clear after successfully passing through the backyard, the gang is feeling a little better. But they know the journey still isn't quite over.

Mike turns to Cruz and asks, "Did you see 'em?"

"No," replies Cruz in a confused tone as Mike looks back at him equally confused.

The gang pauses for a moment and then, as Mike takes a first step onward, they hear the same noise they heard from the house earlier in the evening! Mike stops immediately in panic and turns around to see the shadow behind them!

Seeing it themselves, Phil and Mooch yell, "RUN!"

Turning forward, Mike begins to advance but then sees an image emerging from the darkness into the dim moonlight now barely peering through the heavy clouds. The image quickly darts through the opening in the fence toward Mike, startling him backward, and then races past, disappearing into the backyard. It was the black cat again! Mooch catches Mike, stopping his momentum and then instinctively shoves him forward in fear, desperately wanting to escape. Regaining his balance, Mike charges forward as fast as he can toward the Clarks' front gate. The noise from the house is growing louder. Running for their lives, the terrified Phil, Cruz, and Mooch follow behind him. Scrambling toward the broken gate, Mike dives through feet first, as if he were sliding into home plate, and then rolls safely onto the sidewalk. Cruz and Phil are right behind and land in a pile on top of Mike. Mooch comes through a few moments later, collapses on the ground next to them, and gasps for air.

After a few moments to catch their breaths, they pick themselves up, brush off their clothes, and look at each other, relieved to have made it out alive. As Mooch groans about doing so much running, Cruz remains on the ground, holding his left knee and wincing in pain—he bashed it on the gate diving through. Mike places his hand on Cruz's shoulder, silently asking if he's okay. Cruz nods that he'll be fine. Mike turns toward Mooch to make sure he's okay as well. Mooch nods that he's also fine but then abruptly opens his eyes wide in fear when he sees Josh emerging through the entry gate. He's followed closely by his goons, but now just two of them—Bobby and Travis. Brock is nowhere to be seen—thankfully he must have gotten bored with this nonsense.

As the crew completes their passage through the gate, Mike notices that their costumes are covered with grass and mud stains—

they must have fallen in the hole! They also look alarmed, as if they've seen a ghost.

"There's some kind of scary animal in that yard! It almost got us!" screams Bobby, as they all look back into the yard in fear.

Josh, still partially out of breath and visibly rattled, gathers himself and looks over at Cruz. Seeing the gang's muscle on the sidewalk grasping his knee in pain, he figures this is his opportunity to act and screams out, "Hendricks! Give us your candy bags, NOW!"

"Why would we do that?" asks Mike.

"Because if you don't, we'll hurt you. *Bad*," replies Josh.

"It's payback time," adds Bobby, as the crew members quickly remove and load slingshots from their bags. They each aim at a different standing member of the gang.

"Really? This again?" says Mooch sarcastically. "You guys totally lack creativity."

Josh laughs arrogantly and replies, "I guess that's what you say when you're the one *without* the weapons. Now drop your bags."

With Cruz still on the ground in pain, the others realize they're overpowered and outmatched. They toss their candy bags on the ground in front of Josh.

"Backpacks too," demands Josh as Travis retrieves the dropped bags. Josh and Bobby still hold their slingshots at the ready.

"That's too much," mutters Travis to himself. In his view, taking the bags is plenty.

As usual, Josh and Bobby ignore his opinion. But this time Josh does at least acknowledge he heard, giving Travis a glare of disgust.

Cruz slowly raises himself up, his bad knee bent and carrying little to no weight. Wincing in pain, he proclaims, "That's not going to happen. Now go before I get really angry."

"You don't look like you're in any condition to be making demands," replies Josh, chuckling as he gestures for them to hand over the backpacks.

Cruz makes a move toward Josh, but stumbles and falls back to the ground—his knee clearly not ready for any kind of confrontation. The combined group remains silent and motionless for a few moments as they wait for someone to make the first move—the gang facing toward the Clarks' house and the crew facing away from it. No one else is anywhere to be found.

Having discreetly taken the can of soda from his backpack during the exchange, Phil begins shaking it behind his back. Demanding one last time for the gang to hand over their backpacks, the crew pulls back to extend the bands of their slingshots to their maximum length. Then, just as Mike begins the speech for compromise he's been crafting in his mind, Phil pulls the can from behind his back. Like a ninja warrior, in one continuous motion, he opens the can, launching a forceful spray that showers Josh and his crew with soda. A masterful move timed to perfection by Phil!

Aaaah-woooh! booms a sound from the Clarks' yard—the same sound they heard at this very spot last year! Disrupted by the soda maneuver and terrified by the sound, Josh and his crew move backward to avoid the soda shower and lower their slingshots to their sides, desperately looking around for whatever made the noise. They take a second to look at each other and make a unanimous silent decision to scram. With the Halloween bags they've already confiscated in hand, they bolt down the road.

The gang is equally terrified by the sound and rushes to help Cruz to his feet. As they commence their escape, they stop abruptly when Lisa and Roni step out from behind one of the Clarks' rectangular white-brick fence pillars. Lisa is holding some type of small horn.

Slowly piecing it all together, the gang realizes that *they* made the *aaaah-woooh!* tonight, just as they must have done last year! The boys gaze upon the girls with high appreciation and admiration.

"Thanks! You did that just in the nick of time!" says Mike.

"You're very welcome, Mikey!" replies Lisa proudly.

They all laugh as they watch Josh and his minions run away into the distance. They mingle and recount the excitement of what just happened, each telling their version of the story and listening to the others.

Laughing and celebrating as they cement new memories, a voice suddenly booms from inside the Clarks' yard.

"What's all the commotion out there?!"

They turn their heads toward the gate to see a large dark figure appearing through it. As the figure steps into the moonlight, the group sees it's an old man staring back at them with a confused and concerned look on his face. He's wearing a fedora with a single feather sticking out from the top. It's the shadow! The feather must have been the horn they thought they saw earlier!

"Is everyone okay? I heard quite a bit of screaming—too much even for Halloween. I thought I should come out and make sure no one is hurt. It's been quite a hectic night around here, lots of noise and commotion earlier in my backyard. I guess all the 'monsters' are out tonight, huh?" The old man chuckles.

The kids remain motionless as they stare at the unfamiliar man who's emerged from the haunted house.

"I'll take that as a yes then. My name is Henry, Henry Clark—I own this house. Came down today to check it out and see how everything's holding up. I haven't been here in ages—ever since my beloved wife died of a nasty illness years ago. I just haven't been able to talk myself into coming back—been staying with my brother in Arizona. I miss this neighborhood though, comfortable and quiet—well, at least most nights. But there I go jabbering on. I have a tendency to do that. Where are my manners? What, may I ask, are your names?"

The kids, equally relieved and amazed by what he's just conveyed, begin to chat with Mr. Clark. They tell him the tales of their night, and he shares some from his days as a "young lad" trick-or-treating. They discover all the horrible stories they've heard over the years about this man are completely untrue—he's as nice as can be! They talk a while longer, the kids laughing at Mr. Clark's silly jokes.

Mr. Clark asks if by chance they have a Clark Bar.

"Being named after me, they're, by default, my favorite," he says with a wink.

Mike quickly searches his backpack, finds one, and hands it to Mr. Clark.

"I love these! The perfect combination of chocolaty, chewy, and crispy goodness," he says as he takes a bite and softly moans in approval.

Mooch nods in agreement as the rest of the gang admits their relief of finally being able to enjoy these delicious candy bars. As they say their good-byes to Mr. Clark, Mooch grabs another Clark Bar from his bag and gives it to Mr. Clark as a friendly parting gesture.

Mr. Clark tips the brim of his hat to Mooch. "Good night, all. Have a safe journey home," he says before vanishing through the gate into the darkness.

Having run far enough from the Clarks' house to feel safe, Josh and his crew stop to congratulate each other on stealing a large portion of the gang's candy for the second time. They brag loudly about how they *ruthlessly* and *viciously* stole the candy from Mike's *weak* and *stupid* gang, how they have done this *so many* times before, and how they plan to continue this tradition for years to come. As they round the corner, they see the PC Pack (both kids and parents) staring back at them in disgust and disbelief.

"Joshua Pealy! I can't believe my ears!" exclaims Mrs. Brath. "Your mother will NOT be happy to hear this."

The Zaleznys and Deebles shake their heads in utter disappointment as well.

Curtis, Thomas, and Sebastian are elated. After years of torment by Josh and his crew, they relish seeing Josh expose his true colors to adults. *It's about time!* Awash in satisfaction, they can't help themselves from bursting out loud in laughter and exchanging celebratory high fives.

A pale-faced Josh is horrified—this is not good. Mrs. Zalezny and Mrs. Deeble are *the* gossip queens of the neighborhood. *Everyone* will soon know what he did, *everyone* will soon know his true colors. His good-boy cover is blown. He tries to talk his way out of the predicament, implementing his most-tested manipulation tactics, but it's pointless. They heard every incriminating word he said.

The group turns and walks away into the night, taking Josh's newly discovered true personality with them.

Sulking, Josh thinks, *At least we got a good portion of the gang's candy.*

With his mind on the same thing, Bobby opens one of the gang's bags and finds it full of undesirable candy and rocks—not a single piece of "good" candy!

"Guys, I think we've been tricked again—my bag is full of crappy candy and rocks!" he shouts in disbelief.

The others each quickly grab one of the stolen bags and look inside them to make the same discovery.

Josh is beside himself, thinking, *The night is a complete failure, an utter disappointment.* As he lumbers home, he realizes he's been badly outsmarted by Mike and his gang tonight. He dreads the coming days. All the parents and teachers will finally learn that, despite his upstanding-young-man act, he's actually a malicious, manipulative bully.

Heading back home from the Clarks' house, the girls hand the gang their "real" candy bags, the final move in their successful and ultimate duping of Josh and his crew. While saying their good-byes at the Clarks' back fence earlier, the gang covertly took out the removable "good-candy compartments" from their bags and gave them to the girls for safekeeping. As they'd planned in case of just such an emergency, the remaining nonremovable compartment of their custom trick-or-treating bags contained all the "bad candy" accumulated throughout the night. Just before entering through the hole in the Clarks' fence, they'd quickly added a few handfuls of rocks to make the weight of the bags feel more realistic. Arguably the most masterful plan ever conceived and executed by the gang.

29

That's a Wrap

The combined group of Mike's and Lisa's gangs continue to tell stories about all the happenings of the night as they walk home. One is about how Mooch duped Terry by supposedly leaking the location of their candy stash. As expected, Terry shared this information with Josh's Crew, which set up a distraction assisting the gang to successfully reach Cherry Grove first. While proud of his accomplishment, Mooch is now worried about Terry's reaction to learning she'd been used. He braces himself for her retaliatory wrath. To his surprise, however, Terry expresses her appreciation of Mooch's manipulation tactics and simply smiles at him as she gives a nod of respect. Mooch exhales in relief.

After saying good night to the girls, the gang convenes in Mike's clubhouse to enjoy their favorite candies and trade with one another. Mooch trades his nonchocolate candies for chocolate. Cruz trades for the thickest, most filling candies. Phil stares at the TOTR map, marveling at how well the plan worked. And Mike reads a note he just found in his bag—a note from Lisa that reads "Superman and ~~Catwoman~~ Wonder Woman together next year?" *YES!* Mike thinks as he glances over at Cruz and sees him looking into his bag and smiling. *He must have gotten a similar note from Roni.*

As they continue to enjoy the bounty they've gathered, they recap the night's highlights one last time. They're proud of the plan they developed and the manner in which it was executed. They're completely satisfied with the amazing candy collection obtained, a collection never to be rivaled. They revel in accomplishing the sweet revenge they'd so badly craved against Josh and his crew—and take pride that they did it "the right way." They also reflect on their relief in discovering the true story about the Clarks. All in all, it was a GREAT night—one for the ages!

They know that as they're getting older, their trick-or-treating days are numbered. And with Mooch moving away, they'll never trick-or-treat together again as a foursome. A little sadness creeps into the celebration. They've thoroughly enjoyed every year they've trick-or-treated together, and they collectively wish they could celebrate Halloween as they always have, forever.

Wanting to keep the Halloween spirit alive and feeling they need a new challenge—having just completed the *very best* trick-or-treating outing ever—Phil suggests they focus their efforts on creating the *very best* haunted house ever. Mooch can advise them through letters and over the phone (though the long-distance calls will have to be strategically managed), and maybe he can visit for a day or two to help. The Hantes have a great haunted house, but the gang are confident they can do better. The agreement is unanimous, and they immediately delve into an intense discussion. In their typical manner, they dream up their ideal haunted house in great detail, laughing and joking the entire time. After accumulating a long list of fantastic ideas, while continuing to ingest all the candy they can, it's finally time to call it a night.

They gather their things, walk together to the end of Mike's driveway, and give each other one last round of high fives. Cruz and Phil head out first while Mooch lingers behind.

"I'm gonna miss you, buddy. I'm really gonna miss our Halloween adventures together," says Mike.

"Me too . . . me too," replies Mooch, his eyes welling up. "We sure did have a lot of amazing ones, didn't we? I'll never forget all the fun we had . . . Thanks for being the best best friend anyone could ever have, Mikey."

Acknowledgements

Thank you to Beaver's Pond Press—Lily Coyle and her staff were amazing throughout the entire process! A special thank-you to my project manager and proofreader, Alicia Ester, and my editor, Wendy Weckwerth, for the much-needed wisdom, guidance, and patience provided in transforming my manuscript into this fun-filled novel. Thank you to my design team, Dan Pitts and Deborah Garcia, for your vivid creativity in masterfully extracting the cover style implanted in my mind. I am privileged to have such talented and wonderful people assisting me with this project.

To Jenn—you were the first to join me on this journey and provided me with fresh insight and uncompromising support every step of the way—thank you so very much. To my children—you were with me for much of the journey as well and have given invaluable feedback—thank you. To all my other family members and friends—thank you for all the positive reinforcement and encouragement. I am so thankful to have so many amazing people in my life.

About the Author

Jeffrey Janakus lives in Nevada. He and his family love all aspects of Halloween from trick-or-treating to costume parties to haunted houses. This is his first novel.